General English Proficiency Test

High-Intermediate Level Test ①

Writing Test

Part I: Chinese-English Translation (40%)

Translate the following Chinese passage into an English passage, and write your answer on the Writing Test Answer Sheet.

現在，你不一定要是個全職的學生，才能得到你的學士或碩士學位了。你可以藉由網際網路，就讀線上的大學。在你方便的時候上課，無論是在辦公室、在家，甚至在路上。任何事情，從註冊、選課、買書，到課堂討論、和資料研究，都在線上進行。整體而言，完成課程大約需要兩年。如果你的必修科目較多，或許還要更久的時間。

Part II: Guided Writing (60%)

Write an essay of **150-180 words** in an appropriate style on the following topic. Write your answer on the Writing Test Answer Sheet.

Studies show that people in Taiwan are making slow progress in English learning. Compared to other Asian nations, Taiwanese students receive lower scores on the TOEFL and TOEIC test. Please write A LETTER to the Minister of Education to suggest what you think the government should do to improve this situation.

Speaking Test

Please read the self-introduction sentence.

My seat number is （複試座位號碼）, and my registration number is （初試准考證號碼）.

Part I: Answering Questions

You will hear 8 questions. Each question will be spoken once. Please answer the question immediately after you hear it.

For questions 1 to 4, you will have 15 seconds to answer each question.

For questions 5 to 8, you will have 30 seconds to answer each question.

Part II: Picture Description

Look at the picture, think about the questions below for 30 seconds, and then record your answers for 1½ minutes.

1. What is this place?

2. What kind of occasion do you think it is?

3. What are the people in the picture doing?

4. Have you ever joined in an activity like this before?

5. If you still have time, please describe the picture in as much detail as you can.

Part III: Discussion

Think about your answer(s) to the question(s) below for 1½ minutes, and then record your answer(s) for 1½ minutes. You may use your test paper to make notes and organize your ideas.

What kind of boy or girl will catch your attention? Name some physical features or personality traits that attract you to a boy or girl. Please explain.

Please read the self-introduction sentence again.

My seat number is <u>（複試座位號碼）</u>, and my registration number is <u>（初試准考證號碼）</u>.

General English Proficiency Test

High-Intermediate Level Test ①

Writing Test

Part I: Chinese-English Translation

現在，你不一定要是個全職的學生，才能得到你的學士或碩士學位了。你可以藉由網際網路，就讀線上的大學。在你方便的時候上課，無論是在辦公室、在家，甚至在路上。任何事情，從註冊、選課、買書，到課堂討論、和資料研究，都在線上進行。整體而言，完成課程大約需要兩年。如果你的必修科目較多，或許還要更久的時間。

At present, you don't have to be a full-time student to earn your bachelor's or master's degree. You can enroll in an online university via the Internet. Attend classes at your convenience, in the office, at home, or even on the road. Everything from registration, course selection and book buying to class discussions and information research is conducted online. On the whole, it takes about two years to finish the program. If you take more required courses, you may spend a longer time.

Part II: Guided Writing

Studies show that people in Taiwan are making slow progress in English learning.　Compared to other Asian nations, Taiwanese students receive lower scores on the TOEFL and TOEIC test.　Please write A LETTER to the Minister of Education to suggest what you think the government should do to improve this situation.

A Letter to the Minister of Education

October 2, 2009

Dear Minister Lee,

Are you aware that in the latest survey of TOEFL and TOEIC scores in 16 and 10 Asian nations, Taiwan ranked No. 14 and No. 7?　*Have you ever wondered why* our students, so dedicated to studying English, should perform so poorly?　Something is wrong with our education system.　Taiwan is notoriously exam oriented.　We really need to introduce some fresh thinking into English teaching here.

We are a country that greatly depends on international trade.　*Besides*, we have been trying hard to develop and boost our tourism.　*Thus*, we need more than English reading and writing.　*The importance of* listening and speaking abilities *cannot be overemphasized*.　Without this all-around ability in English, how can we get more involved with the world?

This is a major undertaking that requires government help. Your ministry took a giant leap forward with the introduction of the GEPT in 1999 for both students and workers. ***However***, this is not enough. Many of our students are well trained in what is stressed on exams, ***that is***, to read and write English. What they really lack are chances to interact with native speakers. They are in urgent need of opportunities to practice listening to, ***and above all***, speaking English. ***Therefore***, we truly hope that the policy of placing foreign teachers in all schools will be implemented. They are not to replace the local English teachers, but to complement and strengthen the current training in English that students receive. ***Furthermore***, schools or even communities should provide more English clubs, books or movies, and English-related activities for students and residents.

Moreover, the government should also put public service messages in English on TV, radio, and the Internet, and on the MRT, buses and billboards. Let English be seen everywhere and in every aspect of people's lives. Put everyone in touch with English. ***Then*** Taiwan can become more like the international place we want it to be.

Respectfully yours,

Sandra Tsai

Speaking Test

Part I: Answering Questions

For questions 1 to 4, you will have 15 seconds to answer each question.

Question No. 1: Do you watch your weight? What do you do?

Answers: As a matter of fact, I do.

I count my calorie intake carefully.

I'm afraid I'll get too fat.

I have a sweet tooth.

I also love to eat junk food.

That's why I have to keep an eye on my weight.

I follow an exercise routine.

I play basketball several times a week.

It helps me stay slim and trim.

Answers: I have no particular need to do so.

I'm not obsessed with looking perfect.

I just try to be natural.

I'm not too fat.

I'm not too skinny.

I'm somewhere in between.

Sometimes I eat like a horse.

Sometimes I eat like a bird.

I just eat what I enjoy.

Question No. 2: Do you think of yourself as an optimistic person? Why or why not?

Answers: I'm an extremely optimistic person.

I always look on the bright side of things.

I have a cheerful outlook on life.

I owe my good attitude to my parents.

They raised me in a very supportive way.

My philosophy is that my cup is always half full.

I'm grateful for every opportunity I have.

If I fail, instead of whining, I try harder.

I truly believe tomorrow will be a better day.

Answers: I have to admit that I'm not a positive person.

I've had too many discouraging and disappointing experiences.

I would describe myself as a pessimist.

There is too much evil, greed and hate in our world.

There are too many corrupt people.

It is frustrating to read the newspaper every day.

Look at the countless disasters around the world.

Look at the deteriorating moral values in society.

I really feel gloomy about the future.

Question No. 3: What was the happiest thing you did last year? Why did it bring you joy?

Answers: My most joyful memory was our family vacation.

We took a trip to a Southeast Asian island.

We felt like we were in paradise.

We swam and sunbathed on the beach.

We went fishing and scuba diving.

We left all our worries and problems behind.

The trip was out of this world!

The scenery, the food and the activities were terrific.

Every day was like a dream come true.

Answers: I think it was when I received an award.

I won a competition at my school.

My teachers praised me and presented a certificate to me.

There was a special ceremony.

Everybody clapped and cheered for me.

I felt like I was on top of the world.

My family went out for a feast to celebrate.

Even my little brother gave me a card.

It felt great to make my parents proud of me.

Question No. 4: Describe one of your bad habits and what makes you do this.

Answers: I have a bad habit of biting my fingernails.

I often do it subconsciously.

I do it when my hands are free.

I don't know when I started this habit or why I do it.

I will do it whenever I am pondering something.

It just happens that my fingernails are soft too.

Experts say that many people have such a habit.

Those who do it seem to be a little self-conscious.

This kind of behavior indicates a sense of insecurity.

For questions 5 to 8, you will have 30 seconds to answer each question.

Question No. 5: What is an ideal trip in your opinion?

Answers: I love to be close to Mother Nature.

So I enjoy traveling in a pristine area.

A place with unspoiled natural scenery suits me well.

Urban prosperity doesn't appeal to me.

I am not interested in shopping or theme parks.

I would rather choose a less developed place.

Hiking and camping in the mountains would do.

A few days at a beach would be great.

Doing something thrilling like diving would be best
of all.

Answers: I don't care for less developed areas.

Their lack of hygiene and security worry me.

I feel insecure if I go to these places.

I love to go to a modern place.

My ideal trip would be to Japan, the U.S., or Europe.

All of them are clean, have beautiful sights, and
world-class facilities.

I can enjoy their rich culture and history.

I can enjoy their delicious and safe foods.

These places offer a lot for me to see and to do
without worrying.

Question No. 6: Have you ever been a tutor or taught anyone anything? Describe your experience(s).

Answers: Sure, I've coached others before.

In junior high I tutored my two younger cousins.

I helped them for a year with math and science.

During senior high, I taught my neighbor's kids English.

It felt great to work and earn money.

I felt my own English improved a lot as well.

In college, I got a part-time job at a cram school.

I instructed elementary students in English.

It was a challenging yet very rewarding experience.

Question No. 7: What are the advantage(s) and disadvantage(s) of being the only child in the family? Please explain.

Answers: It seems great to be the only child in the family.

The family has more resources to offer to a single child.

The only child receives all the attention.

The main disadvantage would be loneliness.

It would be sad having no siblings.

It would be a boring, solitary existence.

Parents might spoil an only child.

Or, the child might be exceptionally mature.

It depends on the relationship between the parents
  and the kid.

Question No. 8: Your American friend asks you about dragon boat racing. Tell him or her something about it.

Answers: Dragon boat racing comes from a story.

A patriotic poet named Chu Yuan drowned himself
  to protest his king's tyranny.

People rowed their boats into the river, trying to save him.

They also dropped rice dumplings into the river to keep
  the fish from eating him.

That's why we hold the dragon boat races and eat
  chung-tze, rice dumplings, during the Dragon Boat
  Festival today.

The holiday is also called The Poet's Day, in memory
  of Chu Yuan.

The boat races are very colorful and exciting.

Most major cities hold their own competitions.

There are even teams from abroad that participate in
the competitions now.

Part II: Picture Description

Look at the picture, think about the questions below for 30 seconds, and
then record your answers for 1½ minutes.

1. What is this place?

2. What kind of occasion do you think it is?

3. What are the people in the picture doing?

4. Have you ever joined in an activity like this before?

5. If you still have time, please describe the picture in as much detail
   as you can.

1. This is a picture of a park in a Western country.

2. I think this is a picnic. The people may be co-workers or classmates.

3. They are socializing. They are talking in small groups and some of them are having a drink. Others are standing and it looks like someone is barbecuing.

4. I myself have joined in such an activity. I once had a picnic with my class in high school. We went to a park and everyone brought something to eat or drink. We had a good time that day.

This is a very spacious park with large trees. There are two groups of young people sitting or standing in the shade. In front, four people are sitting on chairs. Each is having a drink, and the only man is smoking a cigarette. In the background several more people are standing near what looks like a table of food or perhaps a barbecue. They are all casually dressed and it looks like they are having a good time.

Part III: Discussion

Think about your answer(s) to the question(s) below for 1½ minutes, and then record your answer(s) for 1½ minutes. You may use your test paper to make notes and organize your ideas.

What kind of boy or girl will catch your attention? Name some physical features or personality traits that attract you to a boy or girl. Please explain.

Like most people, I notice attractive people. So a tall, handsome boy is sure to catch my attention. He does not have to be very well dressed, but he should be neat because that means he cares about his appearance and the impression that he makes on others. On the other hand, he should not be too fashionably dressed because that might mean he is self-centered or vain.

Appearance is not everything, of course. It is more important that he be kind and intelligent. A sense of humor also helps. And he must have a smile on his face. After all, who wants to talk to someone who looks gloomy all the time?

OR:

A beautiful girl is sure to catch my attention. However, I will pay special attention to a girl's outfit. Knowing how to dress properly is very important for a girl. She doesn't have to wear fancy or fashionable clothes, but she must have her own style. A girl's clothing and even the accessories she chooses reveal her sense of beauty. Besides, it is important for her to wear something that fits the occasion.

Appearance is not everything, of course. It is more important that she be kind and intelligent. A sense of humor also helps. And she must have a smile on her face. After all, who wants to talk to someone who looks gloomy all the time?

General English Proficiency Test

High-Intermediate Level Test ②

Writing Test

Part I: Chinese-English Translation (40%)

Translate the following Chinese passage into an English passage, and write your answer on the Writing Test Answer Sheet.

你晚上睡覺會失眠嗎？當你擔心無法入睡、輾轉反側，想找一個舒適的姿勢時，你其實會使心跳加速，更難放鬆。所以在失眠的夜晚裡，你該做什麼呢？別碰安眠藥，因為安眠藥只會使你的問題更加惡化。你可以在睡前喝杯熱牛奶、吃起司或鮪魚。這些食物中所含有的某些物質會幫助你容易入睡、睡得好。

Part II: Guided Writing (60%)

Write an essay of **150-180 words** in an appropriate style on the following topic. Write your answer on the Writing Test Answer Sheet.

Nowadays, online shopping has become very popular. Have you ever bought anything online? How do you feel about this means of purchasing? Please state your opinions and reasons.

Speaking Test

Please read the self-introduction sentence.

My seat number is （複試座位號碼）, and my registration number is （初試准考證號碼）.

Part I: Answering Questions

You will hear 8 questions. Each question will be spoken once. Please answer the question immediately after you hear it.

For questions 1 to 4, you will have 15 seconds to answer each question.

For questions 5 to 8, you will have 30 seconds to answer each question.

Part II: Picture Description

Look at the picture, think about the questions below for 30 seconds, and then record your answers for 1½ minutes.

1. What is this place?

2. Who do you think these people, including the adults, are?

3. What is the female who is kneeling on the right side of the picture doing?

4. What do you suppose the two kids with helmets are going to do?

5. If you still have time, please describe the picture in as much detail as you can.

Part III: Discussion

Think about your answer(s) to the question(s) below for 1½ minutes, and then record your answer(s) for 1½ minutes. You may use your test paper to make notes and organize your ideas.

Nearly everyone has collections of some sort or other. Please describe what you collect, how you get them, and with whom you share them.

Please read the self-introduction sentence again.

My seat number is （複試座位號碼）, and my registration number is （初試准考證號碼）.

General English Proficiency Test

High-Intermediate Level Test ②

Writing Test

Part I: Chinese-English Translation

　　你晚上睡覺會失眠嗎？當你擔心無法入睡、輾轉反側，想找一個舒適的姿勢時，你其實會使心跳加速，更難放鬆。所以在失眠的夜晚裡，你該做什麼呢？別碰安眠藥，因為安眠藥只會使你的問題更加惡化。你可以在睡前喝杯熱牛奶、吃起司或鮪魚。這些食物中所含有的某些物質會幫助你容易入睡、睡得好。

Do you have difficulty sleeping at night? When you are worried about not being able to fall asleep and toss and turn trying to find a comfortable position, you actually increase your heart rate and make it harder to relax. So what should you do on those sleepless nights? Don't touch sleeping pills, because they only make your problem worse. You can drink some hot milk or eat cheese or tuna fish before you go to bed. Certain substances in these foods can help you get to sleep more easily and have a good night's sleep.

Part II: Guided Writing

Nowadays, online shopping has become very popular. Have you ever bought anything online? How do you feel about this means of purchasing? Please state your opinions and reasons.

Online Shopping

Shopping is a popular pastime, but not everyone enjoys pushing their way through a crowded store. Now there is an alternative--online shopping. I have bought several items this way and I feel very positive about the experience.

Online shopping has several advantages. *First of all*, I don't have to leave my home. That means I don't spend time in traffic just getting to the store. *In addition*, I can find a wide variety of goods on the Internet. That makes it easy to compare prices and features. *Finally*, after I make a purchase, I only have to wait for it to be delivered. I don't have to carry any heavy items home with me.

Of course, there are some drawbacks to this method, *too*. I am very careful to buy only from reputable merchants. *Otherwise*, my credit information could be stolen. With a little common sense, I think this means of purchasing is safe enough. *Overall*, I find shopping from home convenient and comfortable.

Online Shopping

Who in this world has not heard of Amazon.com? If you haven't, you must be living in a cave. It is the world's largest online retailer. The diversity of goods and services it offers is amazing. Now millions of other retailers also do business online and this model is growing like crazy.

The Pros: *Firstly*, you can shop conveniently from your own home, whenever it suits you, day or night, 365 days a year. You are not confined to store hours. *Secondly*, you save time and energy plus all the expenses connected with traveling back and forth to shop. *Third*, there are no pushy, rude, or otherwise unpleasant salespeople to deal with. *Finally*, you get to see or browse through a much wider selection than you ever could in a store, and there are even special, deeper discounts for online customers only.

The Cons: *First*, seeing photos of goods is just not the same as being able to touch them. Although quality assurance is now standard operating procedure for online shopping, when it comes to items like clothing, the size, fit, and even color may just not be up to your expectations. Returning and exchanging goods is a hassle, too. *And finally*, and perhaps most importantly, the chance of identity theft increases dramatically when you shop online.

In the final analysis, the pros of online shopping easily outweigh the cons, and the whole process continues to improve as it becomes more and more commonplace. It's the wave of the present and the tsunami of the future. Online shopping is an irresistible force.

Speaking Test

Part I: Answering Questions

For questions 1 to 4, you will have 15 seconds to answer each question.

Question No. 1: Have you gone shopping lately? Describe your experience.

Answers: I went shopping with my mom last weekend.

We went to a major department store.

We had an excellent time shopping.

We went to the store shortly after it opened.

The clerks seemed more attentive in the morning.

There were few customers and we got great service.

I bought myself a pair of shoes and for my nephew a
  stuffed animal as well as toy cars.

After we had lunch at the food court, the crowds grew larger.

So we went home because I don't enjoy being in crowds.

Answers: Last Sunday I went bargain hunting in the shopping district.

I enjoyed haggling with the storekeepers.

I was good at it, too.

I searched for sales and discounts everywhere.

Negotiating over the price was fun and saved money.

My hard work paid off with some super buys.

I bought a pair of sneakers at half price.

I bought some cool shirts at three for the price of two.

I also received some new promotional products for free.

Question No. 2: When your family eats out, what kind of cuisine do you usually choose and why?

Answers:　Actually we have tried various kinds of cuisine.

Taiwan is a paradise for food.

We hope to taste as many kinds of food as we can.

If it is a usual family get-together, we go to a Chinese restaurant and eat Cantonese, Sichuan, or Taiwanese dishes.

For one thing, it is usually reasonably priced.

For another, it is suitable for my grandparents.

If we have something special to celebrate, we will choose to have foreign food, such as Japanese or French.

What is better is that when we go to an all-you-can-eat restaurant that serves all kinds of dishes.

Everyone can enjoy a pleasant atmosphere and eat whatever he or she likes.

Question No. 3: How often do you clean your house? How do you do it?

Answers:　We do a light cleaning every day.

This includes making our beds and sweeping the floors.

Of course we also do the dishes, wipe the counters and take out the trash.

In addition, we do the laundry every two or three days.

We mop the floors, dust, and wipe all the tables.

My father washes his car weekly.

Once a month, we do a thorough cleaning.

We air out the pillows and blankets.

We wash the windows and scrub the whole bathroom.

Question No. 4: If you heard one of your friends speaking ill of another person, what would you do?

Answers: I don't approve of those who gossip.

I also feel it's wrong to speak ill of another.

However, I think I wouldn't do anything.

I wouldn't like to confront my friend.

And I think it's not my responsibility to correct my friend.

If I did, my friend might feel offended.

I would simply keep silent.

I would pretend I heard nothing.

I would just let the mean remark pass.

Answers: I don't approve of those who gossip.

I also feel it's wrong to speak ill of another.

So I would immediately tell my friend to stop.

I'd explain that I'm not comfortable hearing that.

I'd tell my friend it is not polite.

I'd ask my friend not to do it again.

I'd say, "A wonderful person like you shouldn't talk like that.

Criticizing others only belittles you.

Please try to get rid of this bad habit."

For questions 5 to 8, you will have 30 seconds to answer each question.

Question No. 5: In addition to your English textbooks and testing materials, have you ever read any other English publications? Please describe your experiences.

Answers: My dad gets an English newspaper daily.

I often browse through it.

The sports section is my favorite.

Besides, I subscribe to a monthly magazine called "Studio Classroom."

It's interesting, informative and extremely useful.

I study it nearly every day.

My sister also has a monthly subscription to "Reader's Digest."

Sometimes I will borrow it from her.

I enjoy the stories and the many articles concerned with the latest health research.

Answers: No, I have to admit I haven't.

My English ability is not good enough.

My English comprehension is very poor.

The lessons in my textbooks alone are too much for me.

Worse yet, I also have a lot of testing.

I struggle with my poor English every day.

Sometimes I feel like giving up.

I just don't have the aptitude for learning languages.

I study English only for the sake of exams.

Question No. 6: Christmas is not an official holiday in Taiwan; however, more and more people, and especially department stores and shops, celebrate it. Please describe what you have seen or your own celebrations of Christmas.

Answers: In Taiwan, Christmas is a big commercial event.

Many merchants use Christmas to increase profits.

Celebrating Christmas is an effective way to expand sales.

Hotels, stores and clubs all commemorate this holiday.

Restaurants have special Christmas feasts.

Even schools have Christmas decorations everywhere.

We all know Christmas falls on December 25.

It celebrates the birth of Jesus Christ.

Does anyone remember that December 25 is also Taiwan's Constitution Day?

Answers: My family celebrates Christmas even though we are not Christians.

We place a Christmas tree in the living room.

We decorate it with many cute little ornaments.

Christmas is not a holiday here, but each of us manages to come home for dinner on Christmas Eve.

My mother often prepares a special Christmas feast.

Sometimes our relatives join us, too.

We buy and exchange gifts.

We also give each other cards expressing our loving feelings.

Christmas is a time for us to share love and thanks together.

Question No. 7:　Who is your role model and why?

Answers:　My father is my hero.

He was born poor so he barely finished high school.

He started working in a factory when he was 18.

Though he doesn't hold a high-ranking position, he

　works very hard to support my family.

He doesn't want me to get the highest scores on exams

　but he does ask me to be a nice person.

Though he is not well-educated, he teaches me a lot.

He doesn't pressure me to study all the time.

Instead, he encourages me to develop some interesting

　hobbies.

I feel lucky to have a father like him.

Answers:　My big brother is my role model.

I admire him for his versatility.

He is almost perfect in my eyes.

He is excellent in academics.

He is a straight A student.

He is extremely intelligent yet modest.

Besides, he is always cheerful and easy to get along with.

He also has a great sense of humor and enjoys

　helping others.

I hope I can be as nice as he, with a high IQ and EQ.

Question No. 8: What do you think are the reasons for the high crime rate in today's society?

Answers: I think many factors contribute to this problem.

The breakdown of traditional families is one cause.

Many kids of divorced parents fall into delinquency.

Society has become so materialistic.

People have become alienated and confused.

Morality has declined as a result.

Schools seem to lack the ability to instill moral values.

The educational system stresses academics too heavily.

Ethics, public service, and patriotism are often neglected.

Our government is to blame.

The poor economic conditions lead many to crime.

The lack of honest policemen and upright officials is another cause.

The media also contribute to the high crime rate.

They sensationalize criminals and their ill-gotten gains.

Program content on TV also glorifies criminal leaders and their luxurious lifestyles.

Part II: Picture Description

Look at the picture, think about the questions below for 30 seconds, and then record your answers for 1½ minutes.

1. What is this place?
2. Who do you think these people, including the adults, are?

3. What is the female who is kneeling on the right side of the picture doing?

4. What do you suppose the two kids with helmets are going to do?

5. If you still have time, please describe the picture in as much detail as you can.

1. This is a kindergarten classroom.

2. The kids are students and the adults are teachers. Some of them may be visiting teachers because this looks like a special safety class.

3. The kneeling woman is helping a girl put on some kneepads. I think the woman next to her is doing the same thing.

4. Perhaps they are going to learn how to skate or ride a bike. It is hard to imagine that they will do this in the classroom, so maybe they are just learning how to wear protective equipment.

This is a picture of a classroom for young children. There are pictures and a map on the walls and low tables around the sides of the room.

Several children are seated on the floor in a semicircle and one woman is sitting behind them on a chair. There is another woman sitting on a chair near the stage. On the stage are three other women. Two of them are helping children put on kneepads. The children are already wearing helmets.

Part III: Discussion

Think about your answer(s) to the question(s) below for 1½ minutes, and then record your answer(s) for 1½ minutes. You may use your test paper to make notes and organize your ideas.

Nearly everyone has collections of some sort or other. Please describe what you collect, how you get them, and with whom you share them.

I collect dolls from different countries. Each of them is dressed in the traditional clothes of his or her country. I began collecting the dolls as a child. When I was seven, my parents took me to Japan and I brought back my first doll. She is wearing a traditional kimono and I still have her. Since then, I have purchased a doll every time I visit a new country. I have also received dolls as gifts from relatives and friends who travel. I display them on some shelves in my room and share them with my family and friends. They remind me of all the places I have seen and of how diverse the world is. Perhaps someday I will give them to my daughter.

General English Proficiency Test

High-Intermediate Level Test ③

Writing Test

Part I: Chinese-English Translation (40%)

Translate the following Chinese passage into an English passage, and write your answer on the Writing Test Answer Sheet.

成功的人是一個能以幽默感面對挫折的人。世上無人能永遠成功，也沒有人總是失敗。要成功，通常先要歷經一連串失敗的考驗。換言之，能輸得起的人就有贏的希望。持續不斷的努力是你致勝的關鍵。但是必定要記住，勝不驕、敗不餒。被一時的勝利沖昏了頭，你就和你的成功說再見了。

Part II: Guided Writing (60%)

Write an essay of **150-180 words** in an appropriate style on the following topic. Write your answer on the Writing Test Answer Sheet.

There are now many universities and businesses requiring their applicants to pass some kind of English proficiency test, like the one you are taking now. Do you agree or disagree with such a policy? Please state your opinions and reasons.

Speaking Test

Please read the self-introduction sentence.

My seat number is （複試座位號碼）, and my registration number is （初試准考證號碼）.

Part I: Answering Questions

You will hear 8 questions. Each question will be spoken once. Please answer the question immediately after you hear it.

For questions 1 to 4, you will have 15 seconds to answer each question.

For questions 5 to 8, you will have 30 seconds to answer each question.

Part II: Picture Description

Look at the picture, think about the questions below for 30 seconds, and then record your answers for 1½ minutes.

1. What is this place?

2. What are these people doing?

3. What is the difference between the woman on the left and the others?

4. If you still have time, please describe the picture in as much detail as you can.

Part III: Discussion

Think about your answer(s) to the question(s) below for 1½ minutes, and then record your answer(s) for 1½ minutes. You may use your test paper to make notes and organize your ideas.

There are more and more foreigners coming to Taiwan either for sightseeing or for work. What attractions do we have to bring them here? What else should we do to encourage more to come? Please explain.

Please read the self-introduction sentence again.

My seat number is （複試座位號碼）, and my registration number is （初試准考證號碼）.

General English Proficiency Test

High-Intermediate Level Test ③

Writing Test

Part I: Chinese-English Translation

　　成功的人是一個能以幽默感面對挫折的人。世上無人能永遠成功，也沒有人總是失敗。要成功，通常先要歷經一連串失敗的考驗。換言之，能輸得起的人就有贏的希望。持續不斷的努力是你致勝的關鍵。但是必定要記住，勝不驕、敗不餒。被一時的勝利沖昏了頭，你就和你的成功說再見了。

A successful person is one who can face frustration with a sense of humor. No one in the world can succeed all the time, nor will one always fail. To succeed, one will usually go through the ordeal of a series of failures first. In other words, a person who takes defeat well stands a chance of winning. Constant effort is the key to victory. However, make sure to remember that you mustn't be overly proud when you win and that you shouldn't be discouraged when you lose. Let an instant triumph go to your head, and you are saying goodbye to your success.

Part II: Guided Writing

There are now many universities and businesses requiring their applicants to pass some kind of English proficiency test, like the one you are taking now. Do you agree or disagree with such a policy? Please state your opinions and reasons.

English Proficiency Test

Many businesses now require their employees to speak English and universities expect incoming students to have a reasonable command of the language. In order to ensure a certain level of proficiency, they require prospective workers or students to take a test. I agree with this policy, but I don't believe that it should be the only factor in the hiring or admission decision.

Companies and schools need an efficient way to narrow down their number of applicants. If English is an important part of the job or course, then an entrance examination makes sense. It will not only tell the decision makers that the applicant is able to communicate in English but also that he or she is able to prepare well and to handle stressful situations. *Moreover*, a basic test is a fair way to distinguish among the applicants.

However, since English ability is not the only thing that qualifies a person for a position, other factors must be considered. Each person's general intelligence, achievements and personality should also be taken into account. *After all*, if an applicant is good in other areas, it stands to reason that he or she could improve in English.

Speaking Test

Part I: Answering Questions

For questions 1 to 4, you will have 15 seconds to answer each question.

Question No. 1: **When a show that you are looking forward to is canceled, what do you say?**

Answers:　Oh, no, I can't believe it.

It's happened to me again.

The show has been canceled.

Why am I so unlucky?

I think I wanted it too much.

I feel like I've been cursed.

Well, there's nothing that can be done about it.

We'll have to figure out something else for the night.

Maybe we can find a decent movie instead.

Question No. 2: **What do you usually do for English practice?**

Answers:　I listen to ICRT every day.

I also enjoy listening to English songs.

I improve my listening ability in this way.

Besides, I read English newspapers a lot.

I enjoy comic books in English.

I often practice writing English essays.

Most of all, I think it is great to converse face to
face with foreigners.

I never pass up any chance to speak English.

Whenever I go to a McDonald's or Starbucks,
I try to strike up a conversation with a
native speaker.

Question No. 3: **Have you ever thought about studying abroad?**
Why or why not?

Answers: Of course, I've thought about studying abroad.

What student hasn't?

I would love to study in America.

American universities offer a wide range
of courses.

The facilities are state-of-the-art.

The professors are tops in their fields.

Above all, I enjoy the liberal atmosphere on an
American campus.

Besides, I'll get immersed in American culture.

I can take advantage of the opportunity to travel
around the States at the same time.

Answers: There's no way I can study abroad.

It's a total fantasy.

First of all, my English isn't good enough.

In addition, there's also the question of money.

It costs a fortune to study overseas.

My parents just couldn't afford it.

Besides, I am a homebody.

Just the thought of living in a foreign environment makes me feel ill at ease.

It would be hard for me to get used to life away from home.

Question No. 4: Are you a rational or emotional person?

Answers: I am a believer in Descartes.

My motto is "I think, therefore I am."

I try to make every decision rationally.

I analyze before and after I do everything.

I make it a habit to get things organized.

That's why I got the nickname "Robot" from my friends.

Perhaps they think I am a little boring.

However, when they're in trouble, it's me they come to for advice or help.

They know they can always count on me.

Answers: I am an emotional person.

I get touched very easily.

Just a good movie or a nice song may move me to tears.

I believe in following my heart.

I like to be spontaneous.

I'm happiest when I say and do what I am feeling.

If I were less sensitive, I wouldn't get hurt as much as I do.

But it wouldn't be me.

Besides, I'd have missed virtually all of my most
memorable experiences.

For questions 5 to 8, you will have 30 seconds to answer each question.

Question No. 5: Please describe one of your frustrating experiences.

Answers: I love American basketball, especially the NBA.

A couple of years back a famous NBA star was
invited to Taipei.

He came for only one day to demonstrate his skills
and then answer questions.

With great difficulty, my friend and I got tickets for
the exhibition.

We were so excited.

We started counting down the days from 100.

And then it happened.

My sister fell in love and got married in the blink of an eye.

You guessed it—the marriage took place on what
should have been my NBA day.

Answers: I've been interested in math since elementary school.

I was at the top of the class in math.

I even won a math competition in my school.

I was confident that I could get high scores in math.

I had thought it would not be a problem at all in the
college entrance exam.

However, when the college entrance exam did come,
I read the test paper and my mind went blank.

I failed to answer several questions.

I felt extremely frustrated after the test.

It turned out that I got a relatively low score.

Question No. 6: **Would you prefer being at the bottom of an excellent
class or at the top of an ordinary class? Please state
the reasons for your choice.**

Answers: I'd much prefer to be at the bottom of an excellent class.

I would be perpetually forced to strive.

I would be constantly seeking to improve.

Being in this position would keep me on my toes.

Yes, it would be difficult at times.

But the rewards would be tremendous.

I'm sure I would make great progress.

Even if I remained at the bottom, my absolute
improvement would be significant.

I'm sure with diligence I would make my parents
and myself proud.

Answers: I would rather be at the top of an ordinary class.

I believe that would be less pressure.

I would feel less stressed out.

I wouldn't feel inferior to others.

I wouldn't feel frustrated all the time.

That way I would be a happier person.

I could enjoy studying more.

I could enjoy a sense of accomplishment.

I'd be in a position to be helpful to both my
classmates and my teachers.

Question No. 7: Your American friend is going to visit you and you are planning to show him around. Which place will you take him to and why?

Answers: When my friend comes to Taipei, I will first take
him to the latest hot spot in town, Taipei 101.

I decided on this place for a number of reasons.

Right now, right here in our nation's capital, we have
one of the tallest buildings in the whole world.

It is something we Taiwanese can be very proud of,
our latest and greatest landmark.

It's in a definite Chinese style, suggesting a
bamboo stalk.

The observation deck affords a magnificent view of
the city and its environs.

After the manmade masterpiece, I will take him to
　　appreciate the natural beauty of Yangmingshan.
We can enjoy the fresh air and maybe a hot spring bath there.
We can totally relax ourselves.

Answers: My favorite place in Taiwan for a visit is Tainan.
　　　　It is the fourth largest city in Taiwan.
　　　　It is also the oldest city on the island and full of history.

　　　　You can say it is the Kyoto of Taiwan.
　　　　The Confucius Temple is the oldest of its kind in the country.
　　　　There are many famous historic sites, such as the Chikhan
　　　　　　Tower, the Anping Fort, and the Eternal Castle.

　　　　Besides, Tainan is also called "the city of snacks."
　　　　There are many delicious and special foods available,
　　　　　　like eel noodle and coffin toast.
　　　　I think I would also take him to Cheng Kung University.

Answers: I will take him to the east coast of Taiwan, Hualien.
　　　　First of all, we can go to the Taroko Gorge.
　　　　I think it is the most spectacular view in Taiwan.

　　　　Second, white water rafting on the Hsiukuluan River
　　　　　　is very popular.
　　　　I think we can give it a try.
　　　　It must be a thrilling thing to do.

　　　　We will definitely go to the new Ocean Park there.
　　　　We can enjoy the sea lion and dolphin shows.
　　　　Getting close to the dolphins and even swimming with
　　　　　　them is fantastic.

Question No. 8: **What's your opinion of having so many beer and alcohol advertisements on TV?**

Answers: In my opinion, the last thing young people need are
beer and alcohol advertisements.
They give our youth a false impression.
They mislead the youth into thinking that it is cool
to drink beer and alcohol.

Stars from the movies, TV and music sing its praises.
They glamorize alcohol consumption.
But I think it only undermines our health.

I suggest that the government should restrict the
TV hours of these ads.
They had better not be aired in prime time.
Celebrities should not set a bad example, either.

Part II: Picture Description

Look at the picture, think about the questions below for 30 seconds, and then record your answers for 1½ minutes.

1. What is this place?

2. What are these people doing?

3. What is the difference between the woman on the left and the others?

4. If you still have time, please describe the picture in as much detail as you can.

1. This is a stage. It might be in an auditorium or in some outdoor place like a park.

2. The people are playing music. They are members of a band.

3. The woman on the left is singing while the others are not. They are the musicians and she is the vocalist.

It is a picture of a band on a stage. There are four people in the band, three women and one man. One of the women is a singer and the other two are playing instruments, a guitar and a drum. The man is also playing a guitar. They are wearing casual clothes and there are microphones and music stands in front of them. They are probably giving a performance, taking part in a contest, or auditioning.

Part III: Discussion

Think about your answer(s) to the question(s) below for 1½ minutes, and then record your answer(s) for 1½ minutes. You may use your test paper to make notes and organize your ideas.

There are more and more foreigners coming to Taiwan either for sightseeing or for work. What attractions do we have to bring them here? What else should we do to encourage more to come? Please explain.

Taiwan is attracting more foreign visitors these days because it offers several advantages to them. However, with improvements in certain areas, the island could attract even more.

Taiwan has many wonderful features. Most visitors appreciate its natural beauty and friendly people. They also like the convenience of good transportation and communication systems. The country is also politically stable and safe. This all makes doing business and sightseeing here both easier and more enjoyable.

Although the island has many fascinating sights, many potential visitors lack information about them. Therefore, I think we could do more to promote Taiwan abroad and to help visitors discover its unique beauty once they arrive.

General English Proficiency Test

High-Intermediate Level Test ④

Writing Test

Part I: Chinese-English Translation (40%)

Translate the following Chinese passage into an English passage, and write your answer on the Writing Test Answer Sheet.

現代社會中，許多人經常忙到忽略了他們年長的父母或祖父母。有些人不得不將老人送到安養中心，在那兒他們可以找到同伴。但事實上，老人家所需的不只是同伴，還有家人的親情及關懷。老年人奉獻了青春及一生的努力給家庭及社會，因此，年輕的一代應該要心存感激，幫助他們過安詳愉快的生活。

Part II: Guided Writing (60%)

Write an essay of **150-180 words** in an appropriate style on the following topic. Write your answer on the Writing Test Answer Sheet.

When you encounter a difficult question in studying, will you turn to your teacher or your classmate for help, or do you try to solve the problem on your own? On the other hand, if your classmate asks you to help him or her study, what will you do?

Speaking Test

Please read the self-introduction sentence.

My seat number is （複試座位號碼）, and my registration number is （初試准考證號碼）.

Part I: Answering Questions

You will hear 8 questions. Each question will be spoken once. Please answer the question immediately after you hear it.

For questions 1 to 4, you will have 15 seconds to answer each question.

For questions 5 to 8, you will have 30 seconds to answer each question.

Part II: Picture Description

Look at the picture, think about the questions below for 30 seconds, and then record your answers for 1½ minutes.

1. What is this place?

2. Who are the people in the picture? What makes you think so?

3. Have you ever been to such a place?

4. If you still have time, please describe the picture in as much detail as you can.

Part III: Discussion

Think about your answer(s) to the question(s) below for 1½ minutes, and then record your answer(s) for 1½ minutes. You may use your test paper to make notes and organize your ideas.

It is true that the computer brings us a lot of benefits, but there is a growing trend toward computer addiction, which is harmful not only to the computer addicts themselves but also to the whole society. Describe your views about the use of the computer.

Please read the self-introduction sentence again.

My seat number is （複試座位號碼）, and my registration number is （初試准考證號碼）.

General English Proficiency Test

High-Intermediate Level Test ④

Writing Test

Part I: Chinese-English Translation

　　現代社會中，許多人經常忙到忽略了他們年長的父母或祖父母。有些人不得不將老人送到安養中心，在那兒他們可以找到同伴。但事實上，老人家所需的不只是同伴，還有家人的親情及關懷。老年人奉獻了青春及一生的努力給家庭及社會，因此，年輕的一代應該要心存感激，幫助他們過安詳愉快的生活。

In modern society, many people are so busy that they ignore their aged parents or grandparents. Some of them have no choice but to send the aged to nursing homes, where they can find companions. But actually, what the elderly need is not only companions but also the affection and concern of their family. Senior citizens have devoted their youth and lifelong efforts to their families and the society; therefore, the younger generation should be grateful and help them lead a peaceful and pleasant life.

Part II: Guided Writing

When you encounter a difficult question in studying, will you turn to your teacher or your classmate for help, or do you try to solve the problem on your own? On the other hand, if your classmate asks you to help with his or her studying, what will you do?

Overcoming Difficulties in Studying

When I am studying and I run into difficulty, firstly I will try to figure it out by myself because I think it is important to be self-sufficient. I also believe that I will remember the answer better if I work it out on my own. *However*, if I am not successful, I will turn to a classmate or my teacher for help. And I prefer to ask my teacher because I want to be certain that I get the correct answer.

Sometimes my classmates will ask me for help with their studies, too. *In that case*, I always do my best to teach them. I have found that teaching is the best way of learning. Tutoring somebody else helps me to remember and reinforce what I have learned better. *Besides*, it also gives me a chance to help out a friend, which makes me feel great and definitely strengthens our relationship. Perhaps my classmate will return the favor one day.

Speaking Test

Part I: Answering Questions

For questions 1 to 4, you will have 15 seconds to answer each question.

Question No. 1: Do you agree with students working part-time?

Answers: I am in favor of students working part-time.

It introduces them into the adult world.

It helps them develop relationships outside of school.

They learn about responsibility.

Punctuality becomes a serious issue.

So does having a proper appearance at work.

Most importantly, they can earn extra pocket money.

It's never too soon to learn the value of a buck.

They learn to appreciate their hard-earned money.

Answers: I am opposed to the idea of students working part-time.

It will distract students from their studying.

It surely has a negative effect on their school performance.

A student's chief obligation is to study.

School days are the prime time for learning.

Fail to make the best of this golden opportunity, and you
 will be sorry.

Besides, a student working part-time is easily affected
 by the real, ugly world.

He may become materialistic.

He may get infected with the evils of society sooner.

Question No. 2: **Do you prefer watching a movie at a movie theater or on a DVD at home?**

Answers: I'll admit that I'm a bit old-fashioned.

I much prefer watching a movie at the cinema.

There's still something magical when the lights go off.

I love the collective hush of anticipation in the audience as the film begins.

There is something special about sharing the experience with hundreds of strangers.

In a movie theater, I can enjoy the film with undivided attention.

Furthermore, today's blockbuster action films require a large screen.

The special effects, especially through the professional sound system, are amazing on the big screen.

On a DVD at home, too much is lost.

Answers: I prefer watching a movie on DVD at home any day.

I have many reasons to support my feelings.

For starters, I have every comfort within reach in my own living room.

I can watch it with exactly the people I want to be there.

I can eat a messy dessert, have a beer or an apple— whatever I please.

I'm not confined to overpriced popcorn and empty calorie soft drinks.

If I need to use the facilities, I just press the pause button.

In a movie theater, I'd have to miss part of the movie.

Besides, I don't like the acoustics in a movie theater

because I feel they are too loud and noisy.

Question No. 3: In a movie theater, a man's cell phone keeps ringing and distracts you. Please tell him of your complaint.

Answers: Excuse me, sir.

Your constantly ringing cell phone is annoying.

The rest of us are here to see the movie.

The first time I let it go.

Ditto the second.

But this is too much.

Please put your phone on vibrate.

I don't want to hear it again.

If it does ring, I'll be forced to call the manager.

Question No. 4: Your friend is not confident about a promotion. Encourage him to work hard for it.

Answers: I believe in you.

You have all the necessary skills.

You don't need to be afraid or worried.

You are an experienced worker.

I'm certain you can handle the job well.

I'm sure you will be an excellent manager.

Just keep up your hard work.

You deserve the promotion.

It's yours for the asking.

For questions 5 to 8, you will have 30 seconds to answer each question.

Question No. 5: **Who in your family are you closest to and why?**

Answers: I'm closest to my mother.

We two are much alike.

I resemble my mother not only in appearance but also in character.

We have similar attitudes and opinions.

She always understands what I think and vice versa.

Whenever I am in trouble, she is always there for me.

Sure, she spoils me, but only a little.

When she thinks I need a reproach or even a full lecture, she doesn't hesitate.

I never doubt for a second how deeply she loves me.

Answers: I am closest to my youngest sister.

She is four years my junior.

However, sometimes she acts very maturely, as if she were the big sister.

She joins my class gatherings very often.

So she knows my friends very well.

There's nothing we haven't talked about.

We share a lot of common interests and topics.

We have always confided in each other very openly.

I'm sure no matter where our lives take us, we will always remain tight.

Question No. 6: **When planning a trip, would you consider a package tour or would you prefer traveling on your own? Please explain.**

Answers: I like to travel on group tours.

This is the way to get the best deal.

I pay less for the flights, hotels, food and tours than when I travel on my own.

Secondly, there is no wasted time.

The group tour always includes all the must-see places.

It is convenient to travel from place to place on a tour bus.

Everything from transportation to accommodations is well taken care of.

You are assured of good hotels and reputable restaurants.

You don't have to worry about quality.

Answers: I would like to try traveling on my own.

An independent trip has great appeal for me.

I can tour the place at my own pace.

I can go to any place that comes to my mind.

I can sit at an outdoor café sipping a latte.

I don't have to follow the program of a package tour.

Besides, I have more chances of meeting local people.

I can sample the native cuisine.

I may bump into people or things by accident and have some memorable experiences.

Question No. 7: Have you ever had something lost or stolen and how? Please describe your experience.

Answers: My bicycle was stolen when I was in junior high.

I had no one to blame but myself.

I was too lazy to lock it.

My mom asked me to go to the 7-Eleven to pick up some ice cream after dinner.

I thought it would only take a minute.

I ran in, bought it and got my change, and ran out.

When I got outside, I couldn't believe my eyes.

I was completely at a loss.

My beloved bicycle was gone.

Answers: I am a forgetful person.

I often misplace things and then they are gone.

Worse yet, I was once robbed.

On that drizzling night, I walked home alone after a busy and tiring day.

I was kind of distracted and didn't pay much attention to what was going on around me.

Suddenly a man came out of nowhere and grabbed at my handbag.

I struggled to protect my stuff but in vain.

He ran away with my bag after all.

I reported it to the police but received no results.

Question No. 8: **Youngsters nowadays enjoy many more comforts and advantages than did their parents' generation. However, they have lost a lot as well. Please compare the gains and losses.**

Answers: Youngsters' lives today are so different from those of their parents' generation.

On the surface it appears their lives are better in every way.

But have they really only improved?

Certainly in material terms, there is no comparison.

Parents spare no effort to give whatever they can afford to their children.

It seems like every kid has his own cell phone, computer and scooter.

Moreover, youngsters grow up in a better developed and more democratic environment.

They have abundant resources and information to learn from.

Kids now are a lot more intelligent than their counterparts in the past.

However, kids nowadays experience the darker side of society earlier and become mature earlier.

They tend to lose the innocence of childhood.

They also lose a lot of chances to experience a simple life.

In addition, the divorce rate is higher than ever.

More children than before come from broken families.

More youngsters easily go astray without proper

and decent discipline.

Part II: Picture Description

Look at the picture, think about the questions below for 30 seconds, and then record your answers for 1½ minutes.

1. What is this place?

2. Who are the people in the picture? What makes you think so?

3. Have you ever been to such a place?

4. If you still have time, please describe the picture in as much detail as you can.

1. This is most likely a convention room, possibly in a hotel.

2. I think they are business people attending a convention or a seminar, because most of them are dressed in business attire, they are wearing ID badges and there are displays set up in the room.

3. I have never attended a business convention, but I did go to an education fair last year. Many universities set up booths to give students information about their programs.

    This is a picture of a corner of a room in which three tables with displays on them are visible. On the left is a temporary dividing wall with part of the name of a firm of solicitors. This makes me think the convention might be in England or perhaps Australia. There are three people in front of the table. A woman is taking a brochure from the table and two men are talking. Behind them is another display and there are several more people grouped around it.

Part III: Discussion

Think about your answer(s) to the question(s) below for 1½ minutes, and then record your answer(s) for 1½ minutes. You may use your test paper to make notes and organize your ideas.

It is true that the computer brings us a lot of benefits, but there is a growing trend toward computer addiction, which is harmful not only to the computer addicts themselves but also to the whole society. Describe your views about the use of the computer.

I believe that the computer is an important and necessary tool. Without a computer, it would be difficult to keep up with others in business or education. So it is better for people to become computer literate. However, the computer also offers such distractions as online games, chat rooms and so on. Some users become so crazy about these things that they neglect their study, work, friends and family, which in turn causes society to suffer. To prevent this, computer users themselves should exercise self-discipline. Parents can also keep the family computer in the living room, not in their child's bedroom. Then they will know how much time the child spends on the computer and what he or she does. Or parents can be present while their child uses the computer, increasing the interaction with their kid at the same time.

General English Proficiency Test

High-Intermediate Level Test ⑤

Writing Test

Part I: Chinese-English Translation (40%)

Translate the following Chinese passage into an English passage, and write your answer on the Writing Test Answer Sheet.

資源回收是處理垃圾最有用的方法之一。首先，資源回收有助於減少我們每天丟棄的垃圾量。其次，當我們做資源回收，我們就不必蓋那麼多的焚化爐。焚化爐在哪裡都不受居民的歡迎。此外，因為台灣人現在，回收大約總垃圾量的百分之十三，政府就可節省必須用在垃圾處理上的大筆金錢。

Part II: Guided Writing (60%)

Write an essay of **150-180 words** in an appropriate style on the following topic. Write your answer on the Writing Test Answer Sheet.

When you see beggars on the street, do you help them? Why or why not? Please state your reasons.

Speaking Test

Please read the self-introduction sentence.

My seat number is （複試座位號碼）, and my registration number is （初試准考證號碼）.

Part I: Answering Questions

You will hear 8 questions. Each question will be spoken once. Please answer the question immediately after you hear it.

For questions 1 to 4, you will have 15 seconds to answer each question.

For questions 5 to 8, you will have 30 seconds to answer each question.

Part II: Picture Description

Look at the picture, think about the questions below for 30 seconds, and then record your answers for 1½ minutes.

1. What is this place?

2. What do the people in the picture do?

3. What are they doing with the dolphins?

4. Would you like to go to this place?

5. If you still have time, please describe the picture in as much detail as you can.

Part III: Discussion

Think about your answer(s) to the question(s) below for 1½ minutes, and then record your answer(s) for 1½ minutes. You may use your test paper to make notes and organize your ideas.

If you could have a vacation of a whole month, what would you like to do? Would you want to go abroad to travel or study, or just stay at home and spend the time with your family, or something else? Please explain.

Please read the self-introduction sentence again.

My seat number is （複試座位號碼）, and my registration number is （初試准考證號碼）.

General English Proficiency Test

High-Intermediate Level Test ⑤

Writing Test

Part I: Chinese-English Translation

　　資源回收是處理垃圾最有用的方法之一。首先,資源回收有助於減少我們每天丟棄的垃圾量。其次,當我們做資源回收,我們就不必蓋那麼多的焚化爐。焚化爐在哪裡都不受居民的歡迎。此外,因為台灣人現在,回收大約總垃圾量的百分之十三,政府就可節省必須用在垃圾處理上的大筆金錢。

Recycling is one of the most useful ways to dispose of garbage.

To begin with, it helps reduce the amount of trash we throw away

every day. Next, when we recycle, we don't have to build so many

incinerators, which are unpopular with residents everywhere. What's

more, because people in Taiwan now recycle about thirteen percent

of their total garbage, the government can save a huge sum of money

that would have to be spent on garbage disposal.

Part II: Guided Writing

When you see beggars on the street, do you help them? Why or why not? Please state your reasons.

Beggars Deserve Some Kindness

These days I often see poor people begging on the street. I feel sorry for them and I always try to help them out if I can. Some people claim that giving to beggars will only encourage more begging, but I don't agree.

Most of the poor people we see on the streets would rather not be there. Many are disabled and unable to hold a regular job. Perhaps they have no family or their family is very poor. *Either way*, they have no choice but to beg for money. Although what I give is only a small amount, it is better than nothing. If enough people help them throughout the day, then they will have enough to live on.

Giving to beggars is also a way of recognizing their humanity and dignity. Too often they are ignored or despised by the people around them. Who knows what got them into their sad situation? Maybe it happened through no fault of their own. When we acknowledge them with a coin, some food or even just a smile, they will not feel so alone in the world. *Therefore*, I will continue to try to help them.

I Won't Be Fooled Again

Have you ever seen beggars on the street? They must touch your heart a little bit and at least sometimes you must think that there but for the grace of God go I. When you see these people, what do you do? *As far as I am concerned*, I choose to pass them by.

It is not because I am heartless or cruel *but because* I have been deceived a couple of times. *On top of that*, such con games are often reported in the news. Behind these poor people are some immoral ones, who abuse our sympathy and kindness and cheat us out of our money. *Worse yet*, some beggars are not real beggars at all. I once saw a fake crippled beggar walking away merrily after his "job" was over, with the money he had collected and his crutches in his hands. I was furious at the sight of that. I don't want to fall victim to these tricks any more. I don't want to be taken advantage of again.

Of course, I do like to help people in need. I will do this by giving donations to trustworthy charities. *Only* in this way *can I* be assured that my money will go to those who really deserve it.

Speaking Test

Part I: Answering Questions

For questions 1 to 4, you will have 15 seconds to answer each question.

Question No. 1: If you could become any animal, which one would you choose and why?

Answers: Without a doubt, I'd like to be the king of the jungle.

Yes, I'd choose to be a lion.

I would be the master of the animal kingdom.

Virtually every other animal would fear or at least respect me.

I would almost always get my way.

And lions are such noble looking creatures.

Most of the time lions take it easy.

They enjoy themselves in the sun on the plains of Africa.

Hunting for prey must be really exciting.

Answers: I'd like to be a koala bear because it is lazy, just like me.

I've been to the Taipei Zoo to see koalas.

They are so cute.

Koalas only eat the leaves of the eucalyptus tree.

They hardly move at all.

They sleep a lot.

It seems that their lives center on sleeping and eating.

How I envy this kind of idle life.

I think this kind of life would suit me perfectly.

Question No. 2: There are all kinds of cram schools in Taiwan. Do you have any experience of attending one? Please explain.

Answers: Like almost every kid in Taiwan, I've gone to
cram school.
It's a must, especially for high school seniors.
They have to prepare thoroughly for the JUEE.

I attended a very big and famous cram school.
There were literally thousands of students.
It was like a factory assembly line.

I thought I'd be lost in the crowd.
But the teachers and materials were excellent.
Most importantly, thanks to that school, I did very well
on the July exams.

Answers: Of course, I went to cram school.
There's no getting around it.
My parents gave me no choice.

Actually, I shouldn't say that.
Unlike most parents, they allowed me to choose
which one.
And unlike most of my friends, I opted for a small one.

I got to know my teachers very well.
They gave me a lot of individual attention.
I made great progress and exceeded everybody's
expectations on the exam.

Question No. 3: Do you enjoy your life now? Why or why not?

Answers: I am not enjoying my life very much right now.

I am in my senior year of senior high school.

This whole year is devoted to studying for
 the JUEE.

I have no time for my friends.

They, of course, also have no time for me.

My time seems never to be my own.

My waking hours are filled with studying,
 studying and more studying.

My parents are always on my back.

I do, however, realize that my entire future
 depends on this exam.

Answers: I couldn't be enjoying my life more.

Things are going great.

Everything is as it should be.

I have a wonderful family.

We are all extremely close.

We love to do many different kinds of activities
 together.

I find my job very rewarding.

In addition, I have plenty of free time.

That allows me to pursue my hobbies.

Question No. 4: **What do you expect to do in the near future?**
                    Please explain.

Answers: I am certainly going to continue my formal education.

I am definitely going to attend university next year.

I won't know which one until the JUEE results are out.

My dream is, of course, to be accepted at NTU.

That would be just the right start.

In any event, I'm really happy to be finished with
   high school.

Now I'll be able to have a much more well-rounded life.

I want to get back to taking guitar lessons.

Now I'll have some time to go out with my friends to
   KTVs and the movies.

Answers: It's summer now.

For the first time in a few years I will have a real
   vacation.

My whole family is going to the USA.

We are basing ourselves in Los Angeles.

My uncle and his family live there.

We will see all the standard attractions.

I am most looking forward to visiting Universal Studios.

We will also make some weekend side trips to Las
   Vegas and San Francisco.

I can't wait to get going.

For questions 5 to 8, you will have 30 seconds to answer each question.

Question No. 5: **Describe your neighborhood. Do you like living there? Why or why not?**

Answers: I live in a high-rise building in the heart of Taipei city.

It is just a few blocks from Taipei 101.

And it is also quite convenient to the Tong Hwa night market.

I love my neighborhood.

I have so many friends right in our building.

That's why I never mind rainy days.

I've lived my entire life in this neighborhood; in fact, in this very building.

I couldn't imagine living anywhere else.

I honestly think I could spend my entire life here quite happily.

Answers: My family moved to a new neighborhood after my first year of senior high school.

At first, I felt completely lost.

I was like a fish out of water.

I was so settled in my former neighborhood.

I can no longer walk to school.

Now it takes me forty minutes by the MRT and then a bus.

Besides, it's inconvenient in almost every other respect.

It's so far from my favorite specialty supermarket.

But it saves my dad a lot of commuting time and that's most important.

Question No. 6: Do you enjoy reading? What kind of stuff do you usually read?

Answers: I love to read novels, not necessarily the current bestsellers.

I love novels with real character development.

I love to learn about genuine human nature.

I especially love twentieth century American novels.

Give me Faulkner, Fitzgerald and Hemingway anytime.

They are so insightful about people—their motives
   and tendencies.

It doesn't matter a bit that they wrote some eighty
   years ago.

The material world may have changed enormously.

But on matters of the heart people will always be people.

Answers: I'm not much of a reader.

I have so much required reading for school.

When I get a little free time, I want to do something
   very different.

That doesn't mean I never pick up a book.

When I do, it's usually a biography.

I like to learn about my great heroes in more detail.

For example, I just finished a biography of Thomas Edison.

What an amazing range of inventions he created!

He is responsible for so many things of which I was not
   aware, besides his notable inventions.

Question No. 7: Do you have a lot of good friends? What have you learned from them?

Answers: I used to think I had a lot of good friends.

But lately I'm beginning to wonder.

I've been let down by them time and time again.

When a friend asks me for a favor, I do it as quickly as possible.

Recently I've asked some friends for some small favors.

For example, I asked one to give me a phone number and another to pick up a cold drink for me.

I didn't get either one.

From these minor negative experiences has come an important, positive lesson.

Can you count on someone in an important situation who lets you down in insignificant matters?

Answers: I don't have many good friends.

But the ones I have are really dependable.

There's nothing they wouldn't do for me, and vice versa.

True friendship is indeed a two-way street.

You've got to give consistently if you want to get.

When a friend needs a favor, it should automatically never be a "bad" time.

Friends must be loyal and reliable.

You must be able to depend on them.

Friends should always stick up for each other.

Question No. 8: **Chinese Valentine's Day is coming. Do you have any plans for that day?**

Answers: Chinese Valentine's Day is a very romantic holiday.

So, of course, I will be taking my girlfriend out for
a special dinner.

She loves Italian food.

This year I am going to give her a special treat.

I'm surprising her by taking her to an Italian themed buffet.

There's a pasta bar where you can choose from assorted
pastas and sauces.

The appetizers are fantastic.

The choice of main dishes is amazing.

I think she will appreciate the change from our usual
Chinese feast.

Part II: Picture Description

Look at the picture, think about the questions below for 30 seconds, and
then record your answers for 1½ minutes.

1. What is this place?

2. What do the people in the picture do?

3. What are they doing with the dolphins?

4. Would you like to go to this place?

5. If you still have time, please describe the picture in as much detail
   as you can.

1. This is a water park where dolphins perform for people.

2. Because of what they're wearing, I think that they work at the park and are not visitors. I believe the people are dolphin trainers.

3. They are feeding the dolphins. Perhaps it is part of training them to do some tricks.

4. Yes, I like animals and I especially like to watch dolphins.

There are three people in the picture, two men and one woman. They are sitting on the edge of a pool with their legs dangling in the water. They are wearing wetsuits and are feeding and interacting with three dolphins. The dolphins are in the water in front of them. Their heads are out of the water and they are being petted and fed by the trainers.

Part III: Discussion

Think about your answer(s) to the question(s) below for 1½ minutes, and then record your answer(s) for 1½ minutes. You may use your test paper to make notes and organize your ideas.

If you could have a vacation of a whole month, what would you like to do? Would you want to go abroad to travel or study, or just stay at home and spend the time with your family, or something else? Please explain.

If I could have a month-long vacation, I would travel abroad. Normally, it is difficult to get enough time off to travel for very long, so I would definitely take advantage of this opportunity. I wouldn't study formally while I traveled but I think I would learn a lot about other cultures by observing the local people and their way of life. There are many places that I would like to see, so it would be a difficult choice. I might start in Africa because it is very different from my own country. However, I would not go alone. I would go with my family or some good friends. That way we could enjoy the experience together.

General English Proficiency Test

High-Intermediate Level Test ⑥

Writing Test

Part I: Chinese-English Translation (40％)

Translate the following Chinese passage into an English passage, and write your answer on the Writing Test Answer Sheet.

在現代人的生活裡，失眠似乎是個相當普遍的問題。失眠通常會發生在我們有煩惱、緊張或生氣的時候。以我為例，我就曾經失眠。身為一個學生，我過去常常在考試前夕，緊張到無法入睡。然後當我考試的時候，我會覺得昏昏欲睡，而表現得很差。但現在，我已學會盡量放輕鬆，我會努力不讓焦慮影響到我的睡眠。

Part II: Guided Writing (60％)

Write an essay of **150-180 words** in an appropriate style on the following topic. Write your answer on the Writing Test Answer Sheet.

Residents in many Taiwanese cities are required to observe the "keep garbage off the ground" policy. That is, they have to take out their garbage to the garbage trucks at designated time, rather than leave it in outdoor garbage bins. What do you think of this policy? Do you agree or disagree with it?

Speaking Test

Please read the self-introduction sentence.

My seat number is （複試座位號碼）, and my registration number is （初試准考證號碼）.

Part I: Answering Questions

You will hear 8 questions. Each question will be spoken once. Please answer the question immediately after you hear it.

For questions 1 to 4, you will have 15 seconds to answer each question.

For questions 5 to 8, you will have 30 seconds to answer each question.

Part II: Picture Description

Look at the picture, think about the questions below for 30 seconds, and then record your answers for 1½ minutes.

1. What is this place?

2. What do you suppose the people in the picture are doing?

3. Have you ever been to such a place? If not, why not?

4. If you still have time, please describe the picture in as much detail as you can.

Part III: Discussion

Think about your answer(s) to the question(s) below for 1½ minutes, and then record your answer(s) for 1½ minutes. You may use your test paper to make notes and organize your ideas.

Do you read newspapers every day? What section(s) do you like best and what section(s) aren't you interested in? Please explain.

Please read the self-introduction sentence again.

My seat number is （複試座位號碼）, and my registration number is （初試准考證號碼）.

General English Proficiency Test

High-Intermediate Level Test ⑥

Writing Test

Part I: Chinese-English Translation

在現代人的生活裡，失眠似乎是個相當普遍的問題。失眠通常會發生在我們有煩惱、緊張或生氣的時候。以我爲例，我就曾經失眠。身爲一個學生，我過去常常在考試前夕，緊張到無法入睡。然後當我考試的時候，我會覺得昏昏欲睡，而表現得很差。但現在，我已學會盡量放輕鬆，我會努力不讓焦慮影響到我的睡眠。

In the lives of modern people, insomnia seems to be a rather common problem.　Insomnia usually happens when we are troubled, nervous or angry.　Take me for example.　I used to have insomnia.　As a student, I used to get so nervous before a test that I could not sleep.　Then, when I took the test, I felt sleepy and did poorly.　But now, I have learned to relax as much as I can and I make efforts not to let anxiety influence my sleep.

Part II: Guided Writing

Residents in many Taiwanese cities are required to observe the "keep garbage off the ground" policy. That is, they have to take out their garbage to the garbage trucks at designated time, rather than leave it in outdoor garbage bins. What do you think of this policy? Do you agree or disagree with it?

Keeping Garbage off the Ground

In my opinion, the "keep garbage off the ground" policy is necessary in Taiwan's big cities. If people were allowed to put out their garbage at any time of the day, it might go uncollected for a whole day. Given Taiwan's hot climate, this would result in a bad smell and an unclean environment. The garbage would also attract animals like dogs, cats and rats. They might knock over the garbage cans and create a big mess. *Needless to say*, few would be willing to clean it up.

Requiring residents to take their garbage to the trucks themselves also ensures that they separate recyclables from the rest of their trash. A public garbage bin would tempt people to throw in anything they wanted to get rid of whether or not it was the appropriate place. Some people might also place garbage in the bin without the appropriate blue bag. *In the end*, this would create more work for the garbage collectors and make the recycling policy less effective.

Although being required to meet the garbage trucks at a specific time causes inconvenience to some, I believe it is a small price to pay for a pleasant environment.

Speaking Test

Part I: Answering Questions

For questions 1 to 4, you will have 15 seconds to answer each question.

Question No. 1:　To take the test, how did you get to this classroom?

Answers:　I took a bus from my home to the MRT.

After I got off the MRT, I transferred to another bus.

After I got off, I walked to where the test would place place.

A funny thing happened on the way.

I got lost, and I asked a passerby if he knew the way.

He said he did, and he directed me to the classroom.

I told him that it was unnecessary to walk me all the way.

He just replied: "Oh, it's okay.

I'm the test monitor."

Answers:　Getting to the classroom was a nightmare.

I was really nervous the night before, so I didn't sleep well.

In fact, I woke up at least four times during the night.

Of course, not having slept well made me wake up late.

When I woke up, I was shocked to see there was just half
　　an hour left before the test!

I hurried out of bed and ran straight outside.

Needless to say, I took a cab.

The ride couldn't have been slower.

However, I made it to the classroom on time, and that's
　　what counts.

Question No. 2: Have you ever made any special achievements during your school days? Give one example.

Answers: I wasn't an outstanding student during my school days.

I was mediocre not only in my studies but also
in athletics.

However, I was probably the most famous person in my
high school for a special reason.

In high school, I liked a girl in the next class
very much.

It was a secret crush, but soon everyone in my
class found out.

They soon came up with a so-called "fail-proof plan."

During a school-wide meeting, I ran onto the stage and
shouted out my affections for her.

It was a stunt to catch her attention, but she was actually
quite embarrassed.

In the end, I didn't even get to talk to her, but I became
the most famous person in school because of her.

Answers: Dodge ball is without a doubt the number one elementary
school sport.

Like my fellow classmates and friends, I was crazy
about it.

We'd play after school until it was dark.

I was quite good at dodge ball, and I was probably
　　the best player in school.
Because I was so good, my teacher decided to form
　　a dodge ball team with me as the captain.
I was thrilled, and of course I took up the position.

As I look back now, I think my teacher didn't really care
　　that much about forming a team.
He did it just to give me a sense of accomplishment.
I thank him for that, because to this day, it's still an
　　achievement I treasure.

Question No. 3:　Are you a sports lover?　Give an example of one or
**　　　　　　　　　two sports that you like.**

Answers:　I'm a sports maniac.
　　　　　I'm always ready to go on the field and play.
　　　　　If I had to choose my favorite sport, it would definitely
　　　　　　　be soccer.

　　　　　Soccer is the most popular sport in the world.
　　　　　It's a game of stamina, speed, and skill.
　　　　　It's also a game of passion and sportsmanship.

　　　　　I love soccer because it's so exciting and easy to play.
　　　　　All you need is a ball, and you're ready to go.
　　　　　I play it and watch it whenever I have a chance.

Answers: Most people think that sports need to be played on the field.

There needs to be physical contact and pouring sweat.

However, for skinny little guys like me, it's not that appealing.

That's why I fell in love with pool.

There's no sun, no sweat, and no big muscular man trying to run me down.

It's just me, my cue stick, and the pool table.

Outdoor sports require muscles and power, whereas pool requires brains and skills.

Calculating the strength with which to hit the ball is very challenging.

That's why it's my favorite sport.

Question No. 4: Do you have a habit of doing chores at home? What chores do you do?

Answers: I do a lot of chores at home, because both my parents have to work.

I usually split the work with my sister.

I see it as a way to relieve my parents of their pressure after a long day at work.

During the weekdays, I'm in charge of keeping the bathroom clean and tidy.

I also take out the trash every night.

During the weekends, I get to take a break.

I think it's a good idea for everyone in the family to do chores.

It fosters independence.

When we grow up and move out, we will know how to take care of ourselves.

Answers: I don't do chores at all.

Don't get me wrong; I'm not the type of kid who hates
helping out.

It's my mom who doesn't want me to do chores.

My parents put high emphasis on grades, so they wish
for me to study whenever I can.

They think making me do chores is a waste of my time.

So they do all the chores, and expect me to study hard in return.

Sometimes, I'm jealous of kids who have to do chores.

But my friend jokingly told me that I have chores, too.

My chore is to study hard.

For questions 5 to 8, you will have 30 seconds to answer each question.

**Question No. 5: If you could change anything about your room, what
would you change?**

Answers: If I could change anything about my room, I'd start with the walls.

I like bright colors, so I'd change my wallpaper to bright blue.

I'd also put up posters of my favorite bands.

My bookshelf is also kind of old.

I want to buy a new one, and put it beside my bed.

I like to read before I sleep, so it'd be more convenient that way.

Last but not least, I'd like to get rid of the carpet.

It's kind of hard to clean carpet stains, so I want to change
it to a wooden floor.

It would make the room cooler during summer, too.

Answers: I would like my own bathroom attached to my room.

Because there are a lot of people in my family, the line
for the bathroom can get pretty long sometimes.

If I had a bathroom of my own, I'd be able to use it whenever
I wanted.

Secondly, I would get a larger wardrobe.

My collection of clothes has grown so rapidly that I have to
fold them and place them wherever I can find space.

It would be much more convenient if I had a bigger wardrobe.

Finally, I'd like a larger window.

The one I have is rather small, so my room is kind of dark
and gloomy.

I want a bright and sunny room, where I can keep plants.

Question No. 6: Your two best friends are having a fight. Convince them to make up.

Answers: John, I know you are mad at Eric for yelling at you.

But he did so because you were breaking the school rules.

He didn't want you to be punished.

Eric, I know you care about John.

He was doing something wrong, and you tried to correct him.

But next time you should tell him in a better way,
because no one likes to be yelled at.

I believe we are all still friends.

You guys just flew into a temper.

Why don't you make up and talk to each other again?

Question No. 7: Celebrities' scandals and rumors are favorites of gossip magazines. What do you think are their effects on the society?

Answers: Everybody likes to see scandals.

Everybody wants to know about the lives of celebrities.

It's gotten to the point where celebrities have no private life.

Of course, it might be fun for some to see people who they thought were so high above them fall.

However, the frantic search for news and rumors has severely damaged the journalism industry.

The human right of privacy has also been severely violated.

Princess Diana's death is a perfect example of tabloid excess.

Digging for exclusive news hurts not only the celebrities, but also the society.

So I think we should not support this kind of behavior.

Question No. 8: There are many kinds of music. What type of music do you listen to? Who's your favorite artist?

Answers: I listen to different types of music, but my favorite genre has to be hip hop.

There is a special energy to it.

It's an addictive type of music.

The beat is hard and fast.

Some lyrics are funny, and some are serious.

The music varies from slow ballads to upbeat dance tracks.

My favorite hip-hop artist is Eminem.

He is one of the best rappers in the world.

I like him because he writes good lyrics and has a soft
  and sensitive side underneath his tough looks.

Answers: Classical music has always been my favorite.

I've been taking violin and piano lessons since 1st grade.

This has given me the skill to fully appreciate a good song
  when I hear one.

My favorite composers include Mozart, Beethoven, and Vivaldi.

Not only do I love listening to their works, I like playing them,
  too.

It's quite a different experience to hear classics played
  by your own hands.

Classical music, in my opinion, is indeed "classical."

Simply put, it's music for the ages.

No one will ever forget amazing works of art such as
  "Für Elise" and "The Four Seasons."

Part II: Picture Description

Look at the picture, think about the questions below for 30 seconds,
and then record your answers for 1½ minutes.

1. What is this place?

2. What do you suppose the people in the picture are doing?

3. Have you ever been to such a place? If not, why not?

4. If you still have time, please describe the picture in as much detail
   as you can.

1. This is a cybercafé or an Internet café.

2. The people in the picture are playing online games. I can see that there are games on several of the screens and the people are wearing headsets.

3. Yes, I sometimes go to such places to play online games. It's a good way to relax after a hard day, and it's also a challenge to try to improve my score.

   OR

   No, I have never been to such a place. For one thing, I don't have to go to this kind of place because I have my own computer at home. I can do what I like at home. For another, I don't like to play online games. I am not interested in games at all.

   This is a picture of an Internet café or Internet shop. The people in this place are playing games. They wear headsets because some of the games are quite loud, and they are sitting in comfortable chairs because they will probably be there for a long time. The Internet shop is big and very crowded. It looks as though every seat is taken. Interestingly, all of the customers are male.

Part III: Discussion

Think about your answer(s) to the question(s) below for 1½ minutes, and then record your answer(s) for 1½ minutes. You may use your test paper to make notes and organize your ideas.

Do you read newspapers every day? What section(s) do you like best and what section(s) aren't you interested in? Please explain.

I try to read the newspaper every day, but there are some days when I just don't have time. I usually read the headlines first and, if a story sounds interesting, I will quickly read it. I also read the sports and entertainment sections. I like those parts of the paper best because they are interesting and not so serious. I also read the technology section, which appears once a week, because I like to keep up with the latest trends. I can't afford to buy the latest gadgets, but I like to talk about them with my friends.

I don't really like to read about politics but I will read the local news if there is something in it that relates to my life. Otherwise, I find it kind of boring. I also don't care for the business section because I am still a student. It doesn't have much to do with my life right now. But I think in the future I will be more interested in these sections.

General English Proficiency Test

High-Intermediate Level Test ⑦

Writing Test

Part I: Chinese-English Translation (40％)

Translate the following Chinese passage into an English passage, and write your answer on the Writing Test Answer Sheet.

　　大自然是一本能教導我們有關生命本身重要課程的偉大的書。大自然賦予萬物生命；藉由它，我們學到了生命的珍貴。大自然也具有強大的毀滅力；藉由它，我們也學到了生命的殘酷。在此同時，我們還看到在這個世界上的每件事物，是如何相互依賴的。認識大自然是一種開拓心智的經驗。

Part II: Guided Writing (60％)

Write an essay of **150-180 words** in an appropriate style on the following topic. Write your answer on the Writing Test Answer Sheet.

You were an English major in college. You have two years of experience teaching junior high school English. Now you would like to apply to a language school for the position of an English teacher. Please write a letter of self-introduction to the head of personnel.

Speaking Test

Please read the self-introduction sentence.

My seat number is <u>（複試座位號碼）</u>, and my registration number is <u>（初試准考證號碼）</u>.

Part I: Answering Questions

You will hear 8 questions. Each question will be spoken once. Please answer the question immediately after you hear it.

For questions 1 to 4, you will have 15 seconds to answer each question.

For questions 5 to 8, you will have 30 seconds to answer each question.

Part II: Picture Description

Look at the picture, think about the questions below for 30 seconds, and then record your answers for 1½ minutes.

1. What is this place?

2. What do the people in the picture do?

3. Have you ever been to such a place and done what the gentleman in the picture is doing?

4. If you still have time, please describe the picture in as much detail as you can.

Part III: Discussion

Think about your answer(s) to the question(s) below for 1½ minutes, and then record your answer(s) for 1½ minutes. You may use your test paper to make notes and organize your ideas.

Describe one ordinary day of your life, whether you are a student or an office worker. Tell about what you normally do from morning to night and your interaction with people around you.

Please read the self-introduction sentence again.

My seat number is （複試座位號碼）, and my registration number is （初試准考證號碼）.

General English Proficiency Test

High-Intermediate Level Test ⑦

Writing Test

Part I: Chinese-English Translation

　　大自然是一本能教導我們有關生命本身重要課程的偉大的書。大自然賦予萬物生命；藉由它，我們學到了生命的珍貴。大自然也具有強大的毀滅力；藉由它，我們也學到了生命的殘酷。在此同時，我們還看到在這個世界上的每件事物，是如何相互依賴的。認識大自然是一種開拓心智的經驗。

Nature is a great book that teaches us important lessons about life itself. Nature gives life to everything; by means of it, we have learned the preciousness of life. Nature also has great destructive power; by means of it, we have also learned the cruelty of life. In the meantime, we see how interdependent everything in this world is. Knowing nature is a mind-expanding experience.

Part II: Guided Writing

You were an English major in college. You have two years of experience teaching junior high school English. Now you would like to apply to a language school for the position of an English teacher. Please write a letter of self-introduction to the head of personnel.

August 19, 2009

Dear Sir or Madam:

I am writing to you in response to your announcement of a vacancy at your language school. I am currently looking for a new teaching position and your company sounds ideal.

For the past two years, I have been employed as an English teacher at Ren Ai Junior High School. I have enjoyed working with the students and faculty there very much but I am ready for a new challenge. I would like to become more involved with curriculum development and teach a wider variety of students. I understand that the students at your school come from a variety of backgrounds and are learning English for many different purposes. I think it would be interesting to tailor courses for such diverse clients.

With a BA in English from National Taiwan University and two years of full-time work experience, I believe that I would be able to fulfill the responsibilities of a teacher at your school.

Thank for your interest in me and I look forward to hearing from you.

Faithfully yours,

Sandra Tsai

Speaking Test

Part I: Answering Questions

For questions 1 to 4, you will have 15 seconds to answer each question.

Question No. 1: Do you read comics? What do you think about them?

Answers: Yes, I'm a comic lover.

I have hundreds of comic books.

I especially love Japanese comics, or manga.

Comics are easy-to-access books.

With pictures, it's easier to know what is going on.

Most people think they are for kids, but now more and
more adults read them.

I love comics about courage and friendship.

They are the most popular type of "manga," and they range
from ones about ninjas to stories about pirates.

I get all pumped up reading them.

Answers: I don't read comics, and I don't plan to.

I think I am past the age where I need pictures to tell me a story.

I prefer to read the text and use my own imagination.

I'm not saying the authors are not skilled.

In fact, I think it's great to be able to draw a story.

Yet most of the time they lack the skills real writers have.

The language ability of our children has gone down.

I think one reason is comics, because they don't need a
good vocabulary and language skills to read them.

Kids will lose the ability to imagine on their own.

Question No. 2: What's your motto in life?

Answers: My motto is "Live everyday like it's your last."

It doesn't mean you are going to die tomorrow.

It means that you should make the most of everything.

It's important to try hard and give it your best shot.

We don't want to look back and regret not doing
    something.

We want to be able to say: "I did my best and have
    no regrets."

This motto also means you should try new things,
    while you have the chance.

Try to appreciate life as if you could only live till
    the end of the day.

It'll make life much more pleasant.

Answers: My motto is "As you sow, so shall you reap."

I was not born with a silver spoon in my mouth.

Nor am I gifted in many things.

However, I make great efforts.

I take pains with whatever I do.

I believe that success is not possible without effort.

I know that I have no one to rely on but myself.

As long as I work hard enough, I will achieve my goal.

This belief motivates me to keep trying and never
    give up.

Question No. 3:　**Who do you think best represents the Chinese culture? Explain why.**

Answers:　Confucius would be the first choice.

No one has ever affected a culture as much as he has.

He defined many traditional values that Chinese people live by to this day.

Confucius taught the Chinese people respect, compassion, and courtesy.

He also told us about the power of knowledge.

There is a book of dialogues collected by his students and their students.

Confucius affected the Chinese culture greatly, and so did his students and followers.

He also influenced many foreign philosophers.

All in all, without him, we would have a completely different culture and history.

Answers:　Who united the entire Chinese continent?

Who defeated the Muslim world?

Whose army rode all the way to Europe?

The answer, if you don't know, is Genghis Khan.

He was the founder and ruler of the Mongol empire.

It was the largest empire ever.

He was a genius at military strategy, and used smart battlefield tactics to beat his enemy.

He shocked the Westerners, and is well known throughout the world.

He is the most famous Chinese figure, and certainly deserves to represent the Chinese culture.

Question No. 4: Have you ever had a crush on somebody? Did you tell him or her in the end?

Answers: I once had a crush on the girl who sat next to me in cram school.

At first, all I knew was her name and school.

Once she asked me a question, and then we started to chat from time to time.

She had good grades, so I used this as an opportunity to ask her questions.

She always gave me real good answers, although I was never really listening.

She had me looking forward to cram school.

However, I was not bold enough to tell her how I felt.

I just hid my feelings for her deep down in my heart.

I was afraid of being turned down or even laughed at.

For questions 5 to 8, you will have 30 seconds to answer each question.

Question No. 5: Superhero comics and movies have been very popular lately. If you could have a superhuman ability, what would it be and why?

Answers: The best superhuman ability would definitely be flying.

Flying is the equivalent of total freedom.

There is no need to worry about being late or being stuck in traffic.

You have the best view, and there's always enough space.

It takes only a couple of minutes to get from one place

to another.

You could even travel abroad free!

However, I think flying will soon be a regular human ability.

Scientists will make machines that allow us to hover

around freely.

By then, I will have started thinking about space travel.

Answers: Superman can fly and shoot lasers from his eyes and has

super strength.

Spiderman can shoot webs and swing and crawl around.

But I don't want to be like them.

If I could choose a superhuman ability, I would choose

mind control.

With it, I would be able to have my way all the time.

I would never pay a cent, never do homework, and never

have to listen to my parents anymore.

It might sound evil, but I would use it for good, too.

It would be real easy for me to catch criminals.

I would just control their mind and they would turn

themselves in.

Question No. 6: **Brands such as LV, Prada, and Gucci are the favorites of celebrities and the rich. What are your views on brand name worship?**

Answers: Some people buy brand names simply because they are guaranteed products that are of good quality.

However, some people buy brand names because they feel it is vital to their social status.

Those people are the so-called brand name worshippers.

These people have an obsession with buying these expensive brands.

They will do anything they can to get these products, even when they don't have the money.

It's an obsession that affects their normal life.

If you have the money to afford these luxuries, go ahead and do so if you like.

However, if you only make a modest amount of money, save it.

There are other things that are worth far more.

Question No. 7: **In an emergency, you took some money from your mom's wallet without asking. How should you explain it to her when she comes home?**

Answers: Mom, I have to tell you something.

I took some money from your wallet.

Before you get angry, let me explain.

I went shopping with my friends yesterday, and I saw a jacket on sale.

I wanted it really bad, but I didn't have enough money.

If I waited till I got my allowance, the sale would be over.

So I "borrowed" some money from you.

Please forgive me, because to me it was an emergency.

I'll pay you back, with interest!

Question No. 8: Give a few examples of things that foreigners may have difficulty coping with when coming to Taiwan.

Answers: First of all, the weather would pose a problem.

Many foreigners come from countries at high latitudes.

They are not used to the hot and especially humid weather.

Second, some foreigners aren't accustomed to the traffic
　here, either.

There are way too many scooters on the road.

Many riders weave their way through the traffic.

That's why a lot of foreigners I know don't like scooters.

They are so dangerous.

And the roads aren't as wide as in other countries.

Third, the languages of Mandarin and Taiwanese may confuse them.

In some areas, people use Taiwanese more than Mandarin.

Foreigners may not be able to understand or may be
　puzzled by the stress or accent.

Besides, Chinese characters are especially difficult for foreigners.

Each of them is a unique picture.

Foreigners find it hard to memorize or even write them.

Last, foreigners also find some Chinese food very weird.

Chinese people love to eat animal entrails, which
　horrifies some foreigners.

And the famous stinky tofu scares away many foreigners too.

Part II: Picture Description

Look at the picture, think about the questions below for 30 seconds, and then record your answers for 1½ minutes.

1. What is this place?

2. What do the people in the picture do?

3. Have you ever been to such kind of place and done as the gentleman in the picture does?

4. If you still have time, please describe the picture in as much detail as you can.

1. This is the check-in counter at an airport.

2. The man is a traveler. It looks as though he may be traveling on business. The woman works for an airline. She will check his ticket and give him a boarding pass.

3. Yes, I have traveled by plane to Hong Kong. When I went to the airport I also had to check a large suitcase and get my boarding pass.

This is a picture of a large and modern airport. The man, who is wearing a business suit, is placing his suitcase on the scale. The woman will check his ticket, find a seat for him on the plane and issue a boarding pass. I can also see another woman in the background. She is not wearing a uniform, so she is probably a traveler too.

Part III: Discussion

Think about your answer(s) to the question(s) below for 1½ minutes, and then record your answer(s) for 1½ minutes. You may use your test paper to make notes and organize your ideas.

Describe one ordinary day of your life, whether you are a student or an office worker. Tell about what you normally do from morning to night and your interaction with people around you.

I arrive at my office before nine o'clock most of the time. Sometimes I am late because of traffic. The office gets very busy by ten o'clock and at times I feel like the phone is attached to my ear! For lunch, I usually go to a nearby restaurant with my co-workers, but if we are very busy, we will get takeout and eat at our desks. I am lucky because my boss rarely asks me to work overtime, and I usually leave around five o'clock. Sometimes I meet a friend for dinner in town, and sometimes I go home to eat with my family. In the evening, I like to go shopping or see a movie, but if I am tired, I will just stay in and watch TV.

OR

I am a student, so I get up early every morning. I usually leave the house before anyone else in my family has even woken up! After putting on my uniform, I grab my books and head downstairs to the bus stop. It takes me about 20 minutes to get to my school. It is important that I arrive on time because we often have a test in the first class.

After sitting through classes all morning, I eat lunch with my good friends. We like to gossip, so we often chat for the whole hour rather than sleep. In the afternoon I have more classes, and sometimes a PE class. I enjoy that because it is a nice break from the books and it also gives me a chance to exercise. In the evening, I often have dinner with my friends before going to a cram school. If I have no class in the evening, I will go home to eat with my family. Usually I have homework or assignments to do and tests to prepare for. After my work is all done, I like to relax by watching television or surfing the Internet for a while before I go to sleep.

General English Proficiency Test

High-Intermediate Level Test ⑧

Writing Test

Part I: Chinese-English Translation (40%)

Translate the following Chinese passage into English, and write your answer on the Writing Test Answer Sheet.

親愛的約翰和珍妮：

我和傑克將在下星期六下午三點鐘，在我們家，為我們的女兒蘇珊，舉行她十八歲的生日派對。如果你們能帶著你們的兒子彼得光臨寒舍，我們將倍感榮幸。我也邀請了蘇珊的一些好朋友一起來。蘇珊的一位朋友海倫，應我們的要求將在派對上獻唱，還有另一位朋友傑夫會以鋼琴伴奏。而如果彼得也願意將他的小提琴帶來表演一曲，那就太好了。相信我們必能賓主盡歡。我們殷切期待你們的回覆。

羅絲敬上

Part II: Guided Writing (60%)

Write an essay of **150-180 words** in an appropriate style on the following topic. Write your answer on the Writing Test Answer Sheet.

Where do you usually shop for what you need? Do you shop at a department store or a night market, at a traditional market or a supermarket, and what do you buy in these locations? Please describe your shopping habits.

Speaking Test

Please read the self-introduction sentence.

My seat number is （複試座位號碼）, and my registration number is （初試准考證號碼）.

Part I: Answering Questions

You will hear 8 questions. Each question will be spoken once. Please answer the question immediately after you hear it.

For questions 1 to 4, you will have 15 seconds to answer each question.

For questions 5 to 8, you will have 30 seconds to answer each question.

Part II: Picture Description

Look at the picture, think about the questions below for 30 seconds, and then record your answers for 1½ minutes.

1. What is this place?

2. What are these people doing?

3. Have you ever watched such a performance or have your ever taken part in such an activity?

4. What do you think of this kind of activity?

5. If you still have time, please describe the picture in as much detail as you can.

Part III: Discussion

Think about your answer(s) to the question(s) below for 1½ minutes, and then record your answer(s) for 1½ minutes. You may use your test paper to make notes and organize your ideas.

Many department stores hold anniversary sales or year-end sales and, during these periods, they are always crowded with shoppers. Do you like to shop during these periods? Or do you like to shop during usual times? Please explain.

Please read the self-introduction sentence again.

My seat number is (複試座位號碼) , and my registration number is (初試准考證號碼) .

General English Proficiency Test

High-Intermediate Level Test ⑧

Writing Test

Part I: Chinese-English Translation

親愛的約翰和珍妮：

　　我和傑克將在下星期六下午三點鐘，在我們家，為我們的女兒蘇珊，舉行她十八歲的生日派對。如果你們能帶著你們的兒子彼得光臨寒舍，我們將倍感榮幸。我也邀請了蘇珊的一些好朋友一起來。蘇珊的一位朋友海倫，應我們的要求將在派對上獻唱，還有另一位朋友傑夫會以鋼琴伴奏。而如果彼得也願意將他的小提琴帶來表演一曲，那就太好了。相信我們必能賓主盡歡。我們殷切期待你們的回覆。

羅絲敬上

Dear John and Jenny,

　　Jack and I are going to hold a birthday party for our daughter Susan for her 18th birthday at our house at 3 p.m. next Saturday. We would be greatly honored if you could come (to our humble house) with your son Peter. I also invited some good friends of Susan's (to come). One of Susan's friends, Helen, will sing at the party at our request and another friend Jeff will accompany her on the piano. If Peter agrees to bring his violin along and perform a piece of music, that would be great. I believe that all of us will have a great time. We eagerly look forward to your answer.

Sincerely yours,

Rose

Part II: Guided Writing

Where do you usually shop for what you need? Do you shop at a department store or a night market, at a traditional market or a supermarket, and what do you buy in these locations? Please describe your shopping habits.

【Sample 1】

My Shopping Habits

When I need to buy something—whether it's clothing, food or something for my house—I usually head for a traditional market. ***The main reason I go to these markets is that*** the goods are much cheaper there than in modern department stores and supermarkets, but that is not the only reason. I also enjoy the atmosphere.

A traditional market tends to be noisier and messier than a modern store, but, ***in my opinion***, that just makes it lively and interesting. I like to look around at the small stalls. They sell such a variety of goods that I can always find what I need as well as a few things I did not expect. More modern stores rarely surprise me with what they sell. I also feel that the food there is fresher because the vendors buy it straight from the farmers.

The vendors themselves are another reason why I like traditional markets. They are the owners of their own businesses, not just hired workers, so they really care about their customers. They will recognize regular shoppers and make them feel truly welcome. It's fun to stop and chat with them ***as well as*** with the neighbors I often meet there. ***To sum up***, I prefer traditional markets ***not just for*** their lower prices, ***but for*** the way they make me feel part of the community.

【Sample 2】

My Shopping Habits

My favorite place to shop is a large, modern department store. I can find everything I need there from household appliances and furniture to clothes and groceries. It is truly a one-stop shopping experience, which is a convenience I highly value. I don't want to waste my time going from shop to shop or even across town looking for a special item.

Although some people complain that the goods in department stores are high-priced, I don't mind paying more for quality and convenience. *Besides*, I can often find some good bargains during the storewide sales. It's also a wonderful place to browse and see all of the latest fashions, even those I can't afford.

Furthermore, I enjoy the atmosphere. It is air-conditioned, clean and brightly-lit. All of these factors make a department store a pleasant place to spend some time. I often meet my friends there for a shopping spree, a meal or just a coffee. It's a great place to catch up on each other's lives or just sit and people watch.

All things considered, a department store is a wonderful place to spend an afternoon, whether or not I really need to buy something. Shopping in one is convenient, comfortable and fun, and that is why it is my favorite place to shop.

Speaking Test

Part I: Answering Questions

For questions 1 to 4, you will have 15 seconds to answer each question.

Question No. 1: Do you prefer Western food or Chinese food? Why?

Answers: I love Western food.

Steak, burgers, sandwiches, or spaghetti.

You name it—I love it.

Western food is convenient.

You can get a tasty burger and milkshake at a drive thru.

You can buy a sandwich or hot dog from a street vendor.

One reason I like Western food is because of its use
of cheese and sauces like ketchup.

I love the smell of cheese, and the taste of different sauces.

Western food is everywhere, so you'd better get used to it.

Answers: I like traditional Chinese food more than Western food.

Chinese food is an art.

The color, the display, and the taste are all top-notch.

Chinese food is also about being together, a concept that
runs through our entire culture.

Rather than each person eating from his own plate, Chinese
food is for all to share.

That's a big reason why Chinese restaurants always seem
to be quite lively.

My favorite dish is Gong-Pau Chicken.

It is a dish of chicken stir-fried with different spices.

It is spicy, and I always eat a lot of rice when I eat it.

Question No. 2: Do you bargain when you go shopping? How do you do it?

Answers:　I always bargain when I buy things at the night market.

Sometimes I even bargain for gifts at the department store.

If you can get more for less, why not do it?

Some people don't bargain because they feel embarrassed.

But the truth is, most vendors set the prices higher than
　they should be.

You're just wasting your money if you don't make them
　take a few bucks off.

The trick is that you have to make them think you don't
　really need the product.

That way, if you turn away, they will try to make you stay.

That's your chance to cut down the price.

Question No. 3: What's the best present you've ever received? What was the occasion?

Answers:　As a kid, video games meant the world to me.

So on one Christmas, my parents bought me a PlayStation.

I was thrilled and so excited I couldn't sleep the first time
　I played it.

But the best present was one I got when I graduated from
　college.

My parents bought me a car.

To thank them, I took them out to dinner that night in my new car.

A present is a way of showing you care about someone.

It doesn't matter how much the present costs.

It's the thought that counts.

Question No. 4: Which country would you like to travel to? Why?

Answers: If I had the chance, I would like to go to China.

It's the land of our ancestors, the ancient kings and dragons.

It's a land of culture and history, home of the greatest civilization on earth.

China is a big country, so it has diverse environments.

There are canyons and mountains that launch into the sky.

There are deserts, as well as rivers that run deep into the sea.

Ancient Chinese capitals can be seen in their old forms.

Artificial and natural wonders such as the Great Wall and the Yellow River are there, too.

All in all, China is a place worth traveling to, no matter which part of it you go to.

Answers: I would love to go to the U.S.

It is the most powerful country in the world, so it has a lot of big cities.

However, it also has historical sights and natural wonders.

I would love to visit big and modern cities like New York and L.A.

I want to see how the people there live their everyday lives and how they handle living in such a big city.

Of course, I want to go shopping there, too.

National parks such as Yellowstone and Yosemite have great scenery to offer.

The Grand Canyon is one of the most exciting and breathtaking places to visit.

There's so much more I could say about going to the U.S.!

For questions 5 to 8, you will have 30 seconds to answer each question.

Question No. 5: **TV series such as CSI, Lost, and Desperate Housewives have become must-sees. Is there any TV show that you wouldn't miss? Please explain.**

Answers: Reality shows have become a staple on TV nowadays.
The idea of seeing people duke it out for a prize in front of millions of people is really unique.
Who ever thought of it is a genius.

My current favorite reality show is one about supermodels.
The host and judge of the show is world-famous supermodel Tyra Banks.
I have not missed a single episode since the first season.

Why do I love reality shows?
Not only do I get to watch people trying hard to win a prize, I also get to see vicious backstabbing and competition.
These shows really bring a new meaning to the expression "Life is a cabaret."

Answers: CSI is my favorite TV series.
I try to watch it every time it's on.
Even if I miss it, I still have the chance to watch the reruns.

I love stories about law enforcement.
Watching the crime lab investigating all the cases is extremely exciting.
The dialogues and characters are really interesting.

I also learn a lot from this TV show.
Be as careful and thorough as possible in doing things.
Never jump to conclusions without enough evidence.

Question No. 6:　Which traditional Chinese holiday is your favorite?　Please explain why.

Answers:　Traditional Chinese holidays are all so meaningful.
They all represent a part of the Chinese culture.
My favorite has to be the Chinese New Year.

We all know that everyone comes home, and kids get
　red envelopes.
We gamble for fun, and play with firecrackers.
However, that is not the best part.

I love Chinese New Year because of the atmosphere it brings.
People become more polite and forgiving, and we greet each
　other, even strangers.
It's the time of year when we all become considerate.

Answers:　I really love Mid-Autumn Festival.
I think it is the Chinese Christmas.
Westerners have a white Christmas while we have the
　bright full moon.

Moon Festival is also a time for reunion.
All the family members getting together make the home
　full and complete, just like the moon.
Families enjoy moon cakes and pomelos together in the
　pure moonlight.

Besides, this is also a festival full of romantic atmosphere.
I cannot help giving a sigh thinking of the legend of Chang-O
　behind the festival.
What's more interesting is that it has become a holiday
　for barbecue, too.

Question No. 7: **What was the best trip you've ever taken? Who was it with? Where did you go?**

Answers: I once went to the U.S. during summer vacation.

I went with my parents and relatives, ten people in all.

We rented a van, and toured the entire west coast on our own.

We saw the Grand Canyon and Yellowstone National Park.

We went to Las Vegas and had a lot of fun there.

We went to Four Corners, the only place where four states meet.

The entire trip took about ten days.

We came back tired yet satisfied and happy.

It was a trip to remember.

Answers: I just can't forget my high school graduation trip.

We went to Alishan and Kenting.

It was a three-day, two-night trip.

Traveling with friends is always a blast.

We had fun everywhere, not just at the places we traveled to.

In fact, I think we had more fun on the bus and in the hotel.

It was the last big thing we did together before we graduated.

It's a special memory for all of us.

Now I just can't wait for my college graduation trip!

Question No. 8: In recent years, online computer games have become more and more popular. Many young children as well as adults have become addicted. What do you think about this?

Answers: With the Internet boom, it's only reasonable that people start looking for entertainment and friends on the Net.

Internet games provide both of these.

Not only can you play games online, you can also interact with live players instead of just the computer.

However, as with all these forms of entertainment and fun, people get lost and become addicted to games.

This is even worse when it's an online game, because it is a fake world.

When people are addicted to this fake world, they often forget about the real world.

I think it's great that people from all over the world can get together and have fun.

But losing yourself in a virtual game is ridiculous.

Online games need to be controlled, or else they will affect the next generation deeply.

Part II: Picture Description

Look at the picture, think about the questions below for 30 seconds, and then record your answers for 1½ minutes.

1. What is this place?

2. What are these people doing?

3. Have you ever watched such a performance or have your ever taken part in such an activity?

4. What do you think of this kind of activity?

5. If you still have time, please describe the picture in as much detail as you can.

1. This is a gymnasium. It is probably at a high school or university.

2. The girls are cheerleaders and they are leading a cheer.

3. I have seen cheerleaders perform before basketball games. They chant loudly and sometimes perform a dance or some gymnastics.

4. I think cheerleading is fun to watch. It also gets the crowd excited and encourages them to cheer loudly for their team, so it is important to the game.

The cheerleaders are performing on the gym floor. They are wearing T-shirts and shorts. They are in the middle of a cheer and they are holding pom-poms in the air. It is a very large gym and there are many people in the stands waiting for the game to begin.

Part III: Discussion

Think about your answer(s) to the question(s) below for 1½ minutes, and then record your answer(s) for 1½ minutes. You may use your test paper to make notes and organize your ideas.

Many department stores hold anniversary sales or year-end sales and, during these periods, they are always crowded with shoppers. Do you like to shop during these periods? Or do you like to shop during usual times? Please explain.

Oh, I love to go to sales at the department stores because I can always find some good bargains. Sometimes the goods are reduced by as much as ninety percent! I usually look for clothes and other things I need, but I also like to browse. Some deals are so good that I can't pass them up even if I don't really need the item. Some people don't like the crowds that are attracted by these sales, but I actually enjoy them. So many people make the atmosphere more exciting. Besides, it gives me a good chance to people-watch. I only wish that stores had these kinds of sales more often.

OR

I don't care much for the sales at the department stores because the stores will usually become so unbearably crowded. Though the prices of goods in general are reduced, so is the quality of service. Sometimes you have to wait quite a long time to pay. Besides, influenced by the lower prices, we tend to become unreasonable. We may purchase a lot of stuff that we don't really need or buy some discounted clothes in such a rush that we don't bother to try them on, only to find they don't fit well. Shopping at sales often makes me feel full of regret afterwards; therefore, I prefer shopping during usual times in a more leisurely and reasonable manner.

General English Proficiency Test

High-Intermediate Level Test ⑨

Writing Test

Part I: Chinese-English Translation (40%)

Translate the following Chinese passage into an English passage, and write your answer on the Writing Test Answer Sheet.

謙虛是我們中國人重視的美德之一。然而，依我之見，謙虛是一把兩面的劍。一方面，謙虛的人知道人外有人，天外有天，因此他會更加勤奮、努力工作。另一方面，若因過度謙虛而一直貶低自己，反而會使自己缺乏自信心，而妨礙一個人勇往直前。我們應該要在兩個極端之中尋求中庸之道。

Part II: Guided Writing (60%)

Write an essay of **150-180 words** in an appropriate style on the following topic. Write your answer on the Writing Test Answer Sheet.

With the popularity of MP3s and iPods, now you can see many people listening to whatever they like while doing everything from studying to walking to taking public transportation. Do you yourself have such a habit and what do you think of this habit? Please explain.

Speaking Test

Please read the self-introduction sentence.

My seat number is （複試座位號碼）, and my registration number is （初試准考證號碼）.

Part I: Answering Questions

You will hear 8 questions. Each question will be spoken once. Please answer the question immediately after you hear it.

For questions 1 to 4, you will have 15 seconds to answer each question.

For questions 5 to 8, you will have 30 seconds to answer each question.

Part II: Picture Description

Look at the picture, think about the questions below for 30 seconds, and then record your answers for 1½ minutes.

1. Who are the people in the picture? What makes you think so?

2. What is this occasion?

3. Have you ever been to such an occasion?

4. If you still have time, please describe the picture in as much detail as you can.

Part III: Discussion

Think about your answer(s) to the question(s) below for 1½ minutes, and then record your answer(s) for 1½ minutes. You may use your test paper to make notes and organize your ideas.

Many foreigners come to Taiwan and find nightlife in Taiwan, especially in big cities like Taipei and Kaohsiung, really fascinating. What do you think of this?

Please read the self-introduction sentence again.

My seat number is （複試座位號碼）, and my registration number is （初試准考證號碼）.

General English Proficiency Test

High-Intermediate Level Test ⑨

Writing Test

Part I: Chinese-English Translation

謙虛是我們中國人重視的美德之一。然而，依我之見，謙虛是一把兩面的劍。一方面，謙虛的人知道人外有人，天外有天，因此他會更加勤奮、努力工作。另一方面，若因過度謙虛而一直貶低自己，反而會使自己缺乏自信心，而妨礙一個人勇往直前。我們應該要在兩個極端之中尋求中庸之道。

Modesty is one of the virtues that Chinese (people) value. However, in my opinion, modesty is a two-edged sword. On (the) one hand, a modest person knows (that) there is always someone better than him; thus , he will be more diligent and work harder. On the other hand, being overly modest and always lowering himself will make him lack self-confidence and prevent him from moving forward bravely. We should seek a middle course between the two extremes.

Part II: Guided Writing

With the popularity of MP3s and iPods, now you can see many people listening to whatever they like while doing everything from studying to walking to taking public transportation. Do you yourself have such a habit and what do you think of this habit? Please explain.

【 Sample 1 】

Mobile Music

I often listen to my iPod, and I don't think that it is a bad habit. Listening to music helps me pass the time during long bus rides or any time that I have to wait for something. This keeps me from becoming impatient and irritable. *Also*, it can screen out any annoying noises such as car horns or shouting children. *Better yet*, I can use the music to change or enhance my mood. *For instance*, if I am feeling blue, I will take a walk outside and listen to some upbeat songs. I soon find myself walking quickly in step with the music and even singing quietly along. *On the other hand*, if I am upset or angry over something, I will play calm, relaxing music.

People often criticize me for using my iPod when I study, but I don't find the music distracting. *In fact*, certain types of music help me to remember things. *Then*, when I want to recall the facts, I think of the song and they come back to me more easily.

Music is a big part of my life, and having convenient access to it through my iPod is wonderful. It entertains me, calms me or invigorates me as needed. *Therefore*, I am unlikely to give up this delightful habit any time soon.

【**Sample 2**】

The Disadvantages of Mobile Music

IPods and other personal music devices have become very popular. It seems that wherever you look, you see people with earphones. Although it is fine to listen to music now and then, I personally think that this craze has gotten out of control. Listening to music all the time is a bad habit because it may be dangerous or impolite.

We most often see people listening to MP3 players when they are on the bus or MRT. There is nothing wrong with that *as long as* they don't let it cut them off from the world completely. *For example*, some people turn up the volume so high that they cannot hear anything around them. This is very dangerous since they may not hear an approaching car or an emergency announcement, *not to mention the fact that* their hearing will be severely damaged.

Listening to music distracts people from what is going on around them. That is why I don't approve of people listening to music while studying or working. How can they concentrate and do a good job? *Even worse*, some people carry on conversations with others while still listening to their music players. That sends the message that the person they are talking to is not worth their full attention.

In short, while music is an important part of life, it is not more important than other people. We should enjoy it at appropriate times, not all the time.

Speaking Test

Part I: Answering Questions

For questions 1 to 4, you will have 15 seconds to answer each question.

Question No. 1:　What's your favorite movie and why?

Answers:　My favorite movie of all time is "Forrest Gump."
It is a touching and motivating movie.
I have seen it many times, yet whenever I see it on TV
　I still watch it till the end.

The main character, Forrest, is mentally challenged.
He has a devoted mother who gives all her love to him.
The most important thing in his life is the woman he loves,
　who gives birth to his child.

This movie covers almost half a century of American history.
It is told through the eyes of an ordinary yet extraordinary man.
If you haven't seen it, I strongly suggest you do.

Answers:　My favorite movie is not just one, but three movies.
It is "The Lord of the Ring" trilogy.
It is based on an all-time classic by J.R.R. Tolkien.

The movies are an epic, just like the novel itself.
The fantasy story about hobbits, elves, and dwarves fighting
　alongside humans to destroy the ring is captivating.
The cast is great, and the battle scenes are the best ever.

I read the novel first, and I must say quite a lot is taken out
　in the films, but I understand.
The original story was just too big to make into a movie.
However, that doesn't take away from the best trilogy and
　fantasy movies ever made.

Question No. 2: Have you ever been jealous of somebody? What was the reason?

Answers: As a kid, I was jealous of my younger brother.

Everyone in the family loved him because he was really cute.

I felt ignored and sometimes took it out on my brother.

Also, I used to be real jealous of my classmate, Joe.

He always got No. 1 on all the tests, and I was No. 2.

I was jealous of him because he got all the attention from the teachers.

Nowadays I'm hardly ever jealous of other people.

I believe that doing what you are supposed to do is more important than being jealous of what others have.

If you work hard, you can get whatever you want, so there's no point in being jealous.

Question No. 3: Managing our temper is very important. How do you calm down after getting angry?

Answers: There are many ways to calm down.

Some count to ten, while others read or take a nap.

I choose to sit in front of my computer and surf the Web, listen to music, or play computer games.

Surfing the Internet is a good way to distract myself from anger.

I visit one website, link to another, and soon I totally forget what I was thinking about.

Playing video games has the same effect, because I focus on the game instead of my emotions.

I choose to listen to real loud music when I am angry.

Why do I do this?

Because I think I can vent my anger with the noise.

Question No. 4: What's your favorite season and why?

Answers: Spring makes me feel warm and happy.

Although sometimes it rains a lot during spring in Taiwan, overall it is a pleasant season.

And of course, the best holiday, the Chinese New Year, is in spring.

Spring is a time when flowers bloom.

Nature definitely becomes lively.

The grass feels greener, and the air feels fresher.

Spring makes me feel good because it is the beginning of a new cycle.

Just like nature, we are reborn after a whole year.

I feel like working harder in spring than all the other seasons, because that feeling motivates me.

Answers: My favorite season, without a doubt, is summer.

It's the season of sun and good weather.

It's the season of outdoor fun.

To a student, summer means vacation time.

It's a time to go swimming, play sports, and hang around all day with friends.

Of course, there is the bothersome summer homework.

All in all, summer is a time of sweat, sunburns, and tans.

It's a time to relax and have fun.

After summer, we go back to school recharged.

Answers: I love the cool breeze in autumn.

It is not too hot and not too cold.

With summer gone, there is no more heat to make
me irritable.

Autumn is the season for harvest.

I like seeing the red and golden color that covers the
landscape.

It's always a pleasure to take an easy walk after dinner
in the fall.

Autumn also means the end of summer vacation.

It's time to return to school and see classmates and
teachers again.

To me, autumn is a return to life, because it is the
beginning of a new semester.

Answers: Winter is my favorite season.

It is a pity that we don't have snow in Taiwan.

If there were snow, it would be even better.

I don't mind the cold in winter.

Actually, winter in Taiwan is not as cold as in some
other countries.

Even if there is a cold wave, I can always bundle myself
up and keep myself warm.

All in all, I'm a "cool" person.

I don't like the hustle and bustle in hot weather.

I prefer the more laid-back, holiday-filled winter.

For questions 5 to 8, you will have 30 seconds to answer each question.

Question No. 5: Do you collect things? What do you collect and why?
If you don't, what would you like to collect?

Answers: I'm a keen comic collector.

I have more than five hundred comic books.

I preserve each of them carefully on a shelf especially for comics.

It has cost me a lot, but I think it's worth it.

I have some comics in mint condition that should be worth a
lot now.

But of course, I treasure them too much to sell them.

If I had the money and time, I would like to add action
figures to my collection.

They are quite expensive and take up a lot of space, but
I'd like to try.

Having a collection of things is always worth it.

Answers: I have been collecting stamps since I was little.

It was my father who introduced me to this hobby.

I have already filled several albums.

At first, most of my stamps were used, coming from the old
mail my families got.

However, with the popularity of e-mail, letters are getting
rarer.

In the past few years, part of my collection has come from
my family and friends.

They will try to bring me some from wherever they travel.

I also make some exchanges with e-pals on the Internet.

Stamp collecting helps me make more friends and teaches
me to appreciate the beauty of culture.

Question No. 6: **A little girl has gotten lost in the department store and is crying. Help to calm her down.**

Answers: Hey, don't cry.

I'll help you look for your mom or dad.

But I can't help you if you don't stop crying, okay?

Good girl, here's a tissue.

Do you know your mom's name?

Where did you last see her?

I'll bring you to the information desk.

The ladies there will make an announcement.

They will help you find your parents, okay?

Question No. 7: **You're the coach of a basketball team and your team is down by 20 points at halftime. Give your team a pep talk to revitalize them.**

Answers: Guys, I have to admit, we're in a deep hole.

But when a brave man is at a disadvantage, he fights back.

We are brave, aren't we?

When you are on the court, you give it your all.

When you are on the court, you fight till the last moment.

When you are on the court, you strive to be the best and win.

So let's go out and let them know we're not going down that easily.

We are warriors, with one goal, and that is to win.

Come on, team!

Question No. 8: **"Blogs" have become the biggest thing on the Web in the past couple of years. Do you keep a blog? Why or why not?**

Answers: I keep a blog, just like the rest of my friends.

It's a great way to share what you think with people all over the Web.

It's just like a diary, but one you choose to share with others.

I usually update my blog every one or two days.

I write about my day, my thoughts on current events, and sometimes put jokes or videos on it.

It has become a part of my everyday routine to check on my blog.

Keeping a blog also gives me a sense of achievement.

When people reply to what you write or give comments, it's encouraging.

It's a great way to feel that you are appreciated for showing who you are.

Answers: I don't have a blog.

For one thing, I am not so good at computers.

I don't know how to keep a blog.

Second, I am too busy to keep a blog.

If you have a blog, you have to post stuff on it frequently and update it.

That will take a lot of time.

Some people say a blog is like a diary.

But in my mind, a diary is very personal.

I won't share it with other people.

Part II: Picture Description

Look at the picture, think about the questions below for 30 seconds, and then record your answers for 1½ minutes.

1. Who are the people in the picture? What makes you think so?
2. What is this occasion?
3. Have you ever been to such an occasion?
4. If you still have time, please describe the picture in as much detail as you can.

1. I think the children in the picture are the winners of a contest because they are holding prizes. The man behind them may be a judge or their teacher.

2. This is an award ceremony.

3. Yes. My younger brother once won a calligraphy competition and we all attended the ceremony. It was great to see him up on the stage.

The children are standing on a stage. The stage is decorated with very large banners, one of which is a picture of Confucius. They have just won an award and they are posing for pictures. They each hold a box in their hands and are standing in a straight line. A man is standing behind them. I think he is presenting the winners to the audience.

Part III: Discussion

Think about your answer(s) to the question(s) below for 1½ minutes, and then record your answer(s) for 1½ minutes. You may use your test paper to make notes and organize your ideas.

Many foreigners come to Taiwan and find nightlife in Taiwan, especially in big cities like Taipei and Kaohsiung, really fascinating. What do you think of this?

I think many foreigners find the nightlife here interesting because it is different from what they have experienced at home. In cities in Taiwan you can see a lot of people out at night. They enjoy eating out, having a drink together, even window-shopping. Night markets are also a unique part of city life here. When foreigners visit a night market they are often amazed by the variety of goods and food for sale. Needless to say, they are lively and crowded places. There are also more formal performances of traditional music, dance and theater. And, in addition to all that, Taiwan's cities, just like big cities the world over, have a fair number of clubs for visitors to go and explore. There they can often find a unique mix of east and west and easily strike up conversations and make friends with local young people.

General English Proficiency Test

High-Intermediate Level Test ⑩

Writing Test

Part I: Chinese-English Translation (40%)

Translate the following Chinese passage into an English passage, and write your answer on the Writing Test Answer Sheet.

　　對我而言，讀書不只是一種樂趣，也是一種需要。當我想要充實自我、拓展視野時，閱讀是我獲取知識的最佳方法。當我感到無聊時，讀書可以幫助我快樂地度過時光。在各類書籍中，我最喜歡小說，因為小說最貼近我們的生活。以小說裡的人物做為借鏡，我可以學習到許多寶貴的教訓。

Part II: Guided Writing (60%)

Write an essay of **150-180 words** in an appropriate style on the following topic. Write your answer on the Writing Test Answer Sheet.

Fitness centers, spas, and yoga practice are very popular in Taiwan these days. Many people go to these places for a workout or relaxation. What do you think of these places? Have you ever been to one of these places? Please describe your experience.

Speaking Test

Please read the self-introduction sentence.

My seat number is （複試座位號碼）, and my registration number is （初試准考證號碼）.

Part I: Answering Questions

You will hear 8 questions. Each question will be spoken once. Please answer the question immediately after you hear it.

For questions 1 to 4, you will have 15 seconds to answer each question.

For questions 5 to 8, you will have 30 seconds to answer each question.

Part II: Picture Description

Look at the picture, think about the questions below for 30 seconds, and then record your answers for 1½ minutes.

1. What is this place?

2. What do you think this occasion is?

3. Who do you think these people are?

4. Have you ever taken part in such an activity?

5. If you still have time, please describe the picture in as much detail as you can.

Part III: Discussion

Think about your answer(s) to the question(s) below for 1½ minutes, and then record your answer(s) for 1½ minutes. You may use your test paper to make notes and organize your ideas.

Some people don't think women can make good drivers and many people agree that women usually lack a sense of direction. Do you agree or disagree with these assumptions?

Please read the self-introduction sentence again.

My seat number is （複試座位號碼）, and my registration number is （初試准考證號碼）.

General English Proficiency Test

High-Intermediate Level Test ⑩

Writing Test

Part I: Chinese-English Translation

　　對我而言，讀書不只是一種樂趣，也是一種需要。當我想要充實自我、拓展視野時，閱讀是我獲取知識的最佳方法。當我感到無聊時，讀書可以幫助我快樂地度過時光。在各類書籍中，我最喜歡小說，因為小說最貼近我們的生活。以小說裡的人物做為借鏡，我可以學習到許多寶貴的教訓。

　　As far as I am concerned, reading is not just a pleasure but (also) a necessity.　When I want to improve myself and broaden my horizons, reading is the best way (for me) to gain knowledge.　When I feel bored, reading helps me (to) pass the time enjoyably.　Of all the various kinds of books, novels are my favorites, because novels are the closest to our lives.　(By) Using the characters in novels as a mirror, I can learn many precious lessons.

Part II: Guided Writing

Fitness centers, spas, and yoga practice are very popular in Taiwan these days. Many people go to these places for a workout or relaxation. What do you think of these places? Have you ever been to one of these places? Please describe your experience.

The Importance of Fitness

The appearance of fitness centers, spas, and yoga classes in Taiwan is very constructive, *in my opinion*. They provide people with more opportunities to stay in good shape and take care of their health. Their presence also makes the less active among us more aware of the importance of exercise and a positive self-image.

In my own experience, some fitness classes provide a chance for relaxing and socializing. I once took a yoga class at the local YMCA and I enjoyed it very much. The gentle exercise was an excellent way to unwind and relax my mind. Rather than tire me out, the class left me energized, confident and ready to face new challenges. *In addition*, I made several friends in the class. We always chatted cheerfully before and after our lessons.

Perhaps the most valuable thing that spas and fitness classes provide is the time to focus on ourselves. Not everyone enjoys rigorous exercise, but everyone can benefit from devoting some time and energy to themselves. Whether we indulge in a facial and massage or an aerobics class, it is important for us to take care of our mind and body.

Speaking Test

Part I: Answering Questions

For questions 1 to 4, you will have 15 seconds to answer each question.

Question No. 1: **Under what situations do you panic?**

Answers: I'm quite confident of my abilities.

But whenever I'm asked to speak in front of a lot of
people, I panic and get nervous.

As a result, I stutter and can't get my point across.

I also panic when I have to take a test.

This happens to everybody, but I think my case is
exceptionally bad.

I often sweat, my hands shake, and I have to go to
the bathroom.

Besides, I am used to doing things in an organized way.

If things get out of my control, I easily freak out.

I hate getting caught off guard.

I think I get nervous under these situations because
I want to have everything done perfectly.

If I mess things up, I'm afraid I would leave a
bad mark on my record or I would be worried
about how other people look at me.

I have no idea how to get over it.

Question No. 2: What's your favorite course and why?

Answers:　My favorite course has always been math.

People either hate it or love it.

I happen to like it very much.

I love the feeling of accomplishment after solving a really
　　difficult problem.

The process of figuring out the steps and methods to use
　　is good exercise for the brain.

It keeps my mind thinking all the time.

I think the best way to gain interest in a curriculum is
　　not to look at it as schoolwork.

That's how I look at math.

I see it as a way to an intellectual life.

Answers:　My favorite subject is Chinese.

It is often considered a boring and difficult subject.

Yet it is the basis of our entire knowledge and culture.

I think one of the reasons I like Chinese is because I like to read.

Studying Chinese expands my view on literature.

I also get to know more about the thoughts of the authors
　　and the backgrounds of their works.

Besides, studying Chinese is an advantage now.

Chinese is quickly becoming the most important language
　　in the world.

With good Chinese and English skills, I have a good chance
　　to build the future I want.

Question No. 3: Do you believe in love at first sight?　Why or why not?

Answers:　I believe in love at first sight.

Why?　Because I believe that some people are indeed made for each other.

When you see the one, you will know it, so why wait?

It's not unusual to like a person a lot without knowing them well.

Maybe it's the way they speak, act, or look that just catches your attention.

No one can be sure why, but sometimes it just works that way.

All in all, love is a strange thing.

You simply can't explain it in a logical way.

When it does happen, it's a beautiful thing.

Answers:　I have never believed in such a thing.

How can you fall in love with someone you don't know?

How can you fall in love with someone you have just seen or met?

A relationship is built on trust and understanding.

You have to know and accept the other person first.

It doesn't work the other way round.

Love at first sight is something people use as a pickup line.

It just happens in movies, rarely in real life.

A steady and real process is the only way to a successful relationship.

Question No. 4: **If you could have a pet, what animal would it be?**

Answers: If I could have a pet, I'd definitely get an iguana.

It might sound crazy, but I love reptiles.

I've wanted to get one for a long time.

Iguanas are majestic animals; they are like the lion
   of the reptile world.

So it's no surprise that iguanas are usually kept alone.

I think I, too, am a proud person, so I like this
   characteristic in a pet.

They are hard to keep as pets, because of their diet and
   scary looks.

You need to pay much attention to their environment
   to keep them happy and healthy.

But I think that's what makes them so irresistible—you
   need to put a lot of effort into keeping them.

Answers: I would love to have a dog.

A collie would be the best.

I have wanted one since I saw Lassie.

Dogs are humans' most faithful companions.

They have an almost humane nature to them.

They develop a bond with their owners.

Of course a dog needs to be washed, fed, and walked.

It's hard work to keep a dog, but it's worth it.

I would do my best to keep mine in top condition!

For questions 5 to 8, you will have 30 seconds to answer each question.

Question No. 5: Do you know how to dance? Which styles do you dance?
If not, which styles are you interested in learning?

Answers: I started learning ballet when I was five.

The younger you are when you start, the better.

At a young age, the body is more flexible and easier to train.

I trained under a famous teacher until I was fifteen.

Then I moved to a different city, so I stopped taking classes.

I recently started taking classes again, although I'm not back
in top condition yet.

Dancing is a way for me to relax and exercise.

I have also looked into other dance classes.

But I would like to regain my ballet skills first.

Answers: Ever since I saw a breakdancing competition on TV, I have
fallen in love with it.

It's exciting and energetic.

It requires hard practice and extensive training because it is
a real physical dance.

There are many different and acrobatic moves in breakdancing.

They are a mix of smooth body movement and strength.

Seeing a pro breakdance is a real treat.

Some people think street dances such as breakdancing are
for bad kids.

That is not true at all, for breakdancing has become one of
the most popular dances among young people.

I am not a great dancer, but I will work hard to become one.

Question No. 6: If you could choose to be a hero or a villain in a play, which would you be? Why?

Answers: I would definitely choose to be a villain.

I don't like heroes who do everything for "justice."

I think villains are just people who do things everyone wants to do without making excuses for them.

I want to be like my favorite villain, Darth Vader.

He started out as a good guy, but soon his thirst for power overcame him.

Then just before he died, he realized the good in him and saved his son.

DARTH VADER

In the past couple of years, villains have become more and more accepted.

Sometimes, characters usually seen as a "villain" become the heroes.

For example, Jack Sparrow in the Pirates of the Caribbean is a pirate but also the wacky hero.

Answers: There is no need to think about it.

I would definitely be a hero.

A hero is the answer to evil, and defends what is right.

I consider myself a person who is righteous and brave.

I cannot stand other people getting what they want in an unlawful manner.

I think this characteristic will make me a good hero.

However, the society's need for a hero has diminished.

Justice is not as important as power and strength nowadays.

I guess this is why villains are more popular than heroes now.

Question No. 7: What are your views on plastic surgery? Would you undergo plastic surgery if you had the chance?

Answers:　People want to be beautiful, and want to be accepted.

It's a basic human instinct.

Especially nowadays, when good looks often give you an advantage over others.

So of course I can understand why people want to have plastic surgery.

They just want to be attractive when their original looks aren't.

If they have the money and courage, why not?

If I had the chance to have plastic surgery, I'd do it.

I would like to do my lips and make them more "Angelina Jolie," as I like to put it.

I consider her lips to be extremely attractive.

Answers:　I totally disagree with plastic surgery.

Why mess with what your parents gave you?

It's disrespectful and there's also a chance it will fail, scarring you for life.

I think plastic surgery is a social disease.

People are made to think that they aren't good-looking by a standard set by "beautiful" people.

So they have to shell out money to make themselves look like a beautiful movie star.

Beauty is only skin deep, and even more shallow when it's artificial.

I would never have plastic surgery.

I like how I look, and I care more about what's beneath the appearance of others.

Question No. 8: How long do you use the Internet every day and what do you mainly use it for?

Answers: I use the Internet for at least five hours per day.

The computer has become more powerful, and so has the Internet.

I can use it to get just about everything I need.

I download my favorite songs and put them in my iPod.

I google about things I come in contact with.

I also chat with my friends using Skype.

I search for everything I am interested in.

From reports to discussion forums, I can choose what I want to read.

Sometimes I will browse the online shopping sites to see if there is any interesting merchandise.

The Internet is the quickest way to gain knowledge.

A life without the Internet is like a body without hands.

I think as the Internet community grows, my time spent on the Internet will become even longer.

Part II: Picture Description

Look at the picture, think about the questions below for 30 seconds, and then record your answers for 1½ minutes.

1. What is this place?

2. What do you think this occasion is?

3. Who do you think these people are?

4. Have you ever taken part in such an activity?

5. If you still have time, please describe the picture in as much detail as you can.

1. This is a lecture hall. It is probably in a university or a conference center because it is very modern and high-tech.

2. I think this is a meeting of some kind. It could be a university lecture, but there are not many people in the audience. I don't think a small class of students would meet in such a large room.

3. They could be students, but I think they are more likely to be professionals. Most of them are women, so I think they must be members of some female-dominated profession like teaching or nursing.

4. I have attended lectures for my classes, but never in a room as nice as this one. Our lectures are usually in a regular classroom.

This is a meeting hall in which a man is speaking to a small crowd. Most of the people in the audience are women. They are spread throughout the lecture hall and most of them appear to be paying attention to the man. The seats look quite comfortable and there are microphones placed around the room. There is a large screen on the stage with some information projected on it. The man is talking about this information.

Part III: Discussion

Think about your answer(s) to the question(s) below for 1½ minutes, and then record your answer(s) for 1½ minutes. You may use your test paper to make notes and organize your ideas.

Some people don't think women can make good drivers and many people agree that women usually lack a sense of direction. Do you agree or disagree with these assumptions?

I think it is a myth that women make poor drivers. How well one drives depends on one's training and experience. It also depends a lot on patience, and I think women are often more patient than men. It is true that men tend to know more about cars than women do, but that doesn't necessarily make them better drivers. Besides, women can learn about cars too if they wish. Actually, I think that a person's driving ability is an individual thing and it doesn't depend on sex. There are bad women drivers, but there are also bad men drivers. Good driving takes skill and maturity. So I think those who are reckless and disregard traffic rules are the worst drivers, whether they are male or female.

心得筆記欄

心得筆記欄

心得筆記欄

劉毅英文「中高級英檢保證班」

　　高中同學通過「中級檢定」已經沒什麼用了，因為這個證書本來就應該得到。你應該參加「中高級英檢」認證考試，有了這張證書，對你甄試申請入學，有很大的幫助。愈早考完，就顯示你愈優秀。

I. 上課時間： 台北本部： A班：每週二晚上7：00～9：00
　　　　　　　　　　　　　　 B班：每週日下午2：00～4：00

　　　　　　　 台中總部： 每週日上午9：30～11：30

II. 上課方式： 初試課程→完全比照財團法人語言訓練中心「中高級英檢初試」的題型命題。一回試題包括45題聽力測驗，50題閱讀能力測驗，我們將新編的試題，印成一整本，讓同學閱讀複習方便。老師視情況上課，讓同學做聽力測驗或閱讀測驗，同學不需要交卷，老師立刻講解閱讀能力測驗部份，聽力部份則發放詳解，讓同學回家加強演練，全面提升答題技巧。

　　　　　　　 複試課程→完全比照全真「中高級複試」命題標準命題，我們將新編的試題，印成一整本，以便複習，老師分析試題，一次一次地訓練，讓同學輕鬆取得認證。

III. 保證辦法： 同學只要報一次名，就可以終生上課，考上為止，但必須每年至少考一次「中高級英檢」，憑成績單才可以繼續上課，否則就必須重新報名，才能再上課。報名參加「中高級英檢測驗」，但缺考，則視同沒有報名。

IV. 報名贈書： 1.中高級英檢1000字
　　　　　　　 2.中高級英語克漏字測驗
　　　　　　　 3.中高級英語閱讀測驗
　　　　　　　 4.中高級英文法480題
　　　　　　　 5.中高級英語聽力檢定
　　　　　　　　 （書＋CD一套）

V. 上課教材：

VI. 報名地點： 台北　台北市許昌街17號6F（火車站前・壽德大樓）
　　　　　　　　　　 TEL：(02)2389-5212
　　　　　　　 台中　台中市三民路三段125號7F（李卓澔數學樓上）
　　　　　　　　　　 TEL：(04)2221-8861

學習「中高級英檢系列」叢書

適用對象：大學畢業生、商務、企劃人員、秘書、工程師、研究助理、空服人員、航空機師、航管人員、海關人員、導遊、外事警政人員、新聞從業人員、資訊管理人員等。報考大學轉學考試、研究所、托福、多益測驗者，同樣適用。

▶ 中高級英語聽力檢定①②

每冊書+MP3一片 280元

本書共有八回試題，每回測驗分三部份，與教育部公布的範例完全相同。聽力部分要想得高分，反覆練習是不二法門。

▶ 中高級英語字彙420題

書220元

完全仿造「中高級英語能力檢定測驗」中的詞彙題題型，精心設計42回測驗題，提供讀者充分的練習機會，掌握字彙，即是掌握先機。

▶ 中高級英語閱讀測驗

書280元

本書試題全部取材自各大學轉學考入學試題，全書50篇文章，囊括文學、科學、醫學、歷史及生活新知等，內容包羅萬象，充分掌握閱讀測驗命題方向。

▶ 中高級寫作口說測驗①

書+MP3一片 380元

本書共收錄10回完整的中高級複試測驗，並附有解答及回答範例，另附有MP3，讓讀者可以模擬口語練習。

▶ 中高級英文法480題

書220元

文法範圍非常大，但常考的重點有限，只要多做題目，自然能駕輕就熟。本書彙編48回文法測驗題，只要熟記書中所列的文法重點，文法題即可得高分。

▶ 中高級英語克漏字測驗

書280元

試題完全取材自各大學轉學考試題，精確地掌握克漏字出題方向及題型，讀者只要認真練習做題目，必能夠熟悉要訣，掌握重點，實力大增。

▶ 中高級英語模擬試題①

書+MP3一片 380元

每本收錄四回完整的中高級初試試題及詳解，分為聽力和閱讀兩部分，是準備報考中高級英語檢定者的必備書籍。

▶ 中高級英語模擬試題②

書+MP3一片 380元

每本收錄四回完整的中高級初試試題及詳解，分為聽力和閱讀兩部分，是準備報考中高級英語檢定者的必備書籍。

中高級英檢複試測驗①

主　　　編 / 劉　毅

發 行 所 / 學習出版有限公司　　　☎ (02) 2704-5525

郵 撥 帳 號 / 0512727-2 學習出版社帳戶

登 記 證 / 局版台業 2179 號

印 刷 所 / 文聯彩色印刷有限公司

台 北 門 市 / 台北市許昌街 10 號 2 F　　☎ (02) 2331-4060・2331-9209

台灣總經銷 / 紅螞蟻圖書有限公司　　☎ (02) 2795-3656

美國總經銷 / Evergreen Book Store　☎ (818) 2813622

本公司網址　www.learnbook.com.tw

電 子 郵 件　learnbook@learnbook.com.tw

售價：新台幣二百元正

2009 年 11 月 1 日新修訂

ISBN 978-986-231-069-4